Love in the Caribbean
Love and Travel Series

Book 3

Misty Rosette

Copyright © Misty Rosette

This is a work of fiction. Names, characters, places, and incidents either are products of the author's imagination or are used fictitiously. Any similarity to actual events or locales or persons, living or dead, is entirely coincidental

CONTENTS

CHAPTER ONE

The wind in her hair made her feel like she was flying as she walked on the beach sand while jumping and shrieking as the saltwater caught up to her. The scent in the air, coupled with the serene sights in front of her, made her heart full with a feeling she couldn't put into words.

She stopped trying to quantify or put a name to the magic she felt and instead continued running on the sand as she teased the dangerous water body in a game of catch. She didn't go too close. She might have been a good swimmer, but she wasn't ready to test fate.

When she got tired of running, she went under her little umbrella, laid down on a mat to soak in mother nature's essence, but not before she rubbed on some sunscreen all over her body, then reached for the cocktail drink served in a semi coconut and took a deep breath. Perfect. Nothing could be more heavenly; no one could tell her otherwise.

The peace, the quiet, the ambiance, the smell, the food, and so much more. The reason why Jamaica was perfect was not something someone could put into words. To be honest, she wasn't that good at expressing how she felt about anything.

She chuckled, took another deep breath, and sighed. She wished she could show William how beautiful Jamaica truly was, and then he would understand why she wanted them to go there.

Wait?... come here? ...something is wrong? What is it? She couldn't pinpoint what was wrong in her perfect world. *Wait? What is that buzzing sound? What is making that noise?* Disturbing the peace in her dream?

Dream?

Chloe shot up from the bed and sat for a second, looking dazedly around her dark surroundings. This is not Jamaica? Where was she? Her brain wasn't awake yet, but something was telling her that she was nowhere near Jamaica.

Her mouth suddenly felt bitter as she swallowed in disappointment. She was in her flat in London! Chloe might have never been to Jamaica, but for the life of her, she couldn't stop dreaming about the country. It was as if it was calling to her, like an ancestor? She would have laughed. If not for the sudden headache she was feeling.

She wanted to go to Jamaica to see, feel, and be a part of the experience. She just needed to convince William, but that seemed as hard as trying to get him to eat pickles. The man was so scared of the little things.

The sound that had disturbed her dreams earlier was still buzzing. She glanced at her dainty night table beside her bed and noticed that her phone was vibrating.

She reached over for the phone in anger. This person destroyed a perfect dream. She picked up the phone, ready to give the person a piece of her mind, but when she saw the Caller ID, the frown on her face disappeared completely, and she started smiling sheepishly like a baby to a full creamed breast.

Quickly, she pressed the answer button and brought the phone to her ear.

"William? Why are you calling so late?" Chloe asked, blushing like a lovesick idiot.

"Chloe," William said.

Chloe's heart did a double somersault. "This is unfair," she told herself. She was always acting like a fool around William. He knew which of her buttons to push. Just the way he said her name sent her into overdrive, and she couldn't even describe the feeling he evoked in her.

Trying to describe how she felt about her soon-to-be husband wouldn't do the feeling justice. He was an enigma she couldn't understand, no matter how hard she tried.

"Chloe?" William said again, but this time it was a question.

"Yes?"

"You didn't say anything," he said, his voice laced with concern

"You called me; I wanted you to talk...you know?"

"Oh," William said as if something just dawned on him. "I called because of something important."

"Oh really?" Chloe sat up right as if her fiance was right in front of her.

"Yes, I had to tell you something really important." He stressed the importance.

"Just say it already!" Chloe said in anticipation.

"I missed you!"

"Uh?" Chloe's mouth was gaping open with a shocked expression on her face. "...and that's why you called?"

"Wow, here I am filled with love for my fiance, but she doesn't even feel the same way about me."

Chloe opened her mouth to counter his claims, but no good excuse came to her mind. She mentally knocked herself on the head as she pictured William shaking his head like an angry parent to his troublesome ward.

"Wow," he repeated.

"No, no, no... you don't get to play the blame game." Chloe sat up straighter, speaking as if he was right in front of her. "You called this late, and I thought it was because of something import-" she caught herself quickly before he frowned at her again. "I mean, I thought something bad had happened or something, and that was why you called."

"Hmm." William sighed deeply. "I understand perfectly."

Chloe let out a breath of relief. "Thank God, I thought you wouldn't understand."

"Oh, I understand perfectly. You don't want to marry me, and you are looking for a way out. Fine, let's break up."

"Uh?" Chloe jumped on the bed. "What do you mean to break up?"

"I am sorry that I couldn't be the man you wanted," William continued solemnly. "Goodnight."

He ended the call.

Chloe plopped down on the bed. She looked at the phone and then looked at the ceiling. Then she looked at her phone again. Her mind blank, she scoffed, laughing hysterically at the events that had just happened.

After a few seconds, she stopped, laughed, and dialed William's number. The phone rang for a few seconds without an answer. The automated voice came on.

"The number you are trying to call is busy at the moment. Please call back later!"

Chloe stood up, walked to her nightstand like a zombie, and dropped her phone. Then she walked back to the bed and slid under the covers.

One thought flowed through her mind.

It is a dream. When I wake up, it will all be over.

She closed her eyes and slipped into a dream filled with luxurious palm trees, sparkling seas, delicious delicacies, the scent of salt in the air, and peace.

***

The restaurant was almost empty at two in the afternoon, except for an old man in his seventies reading a newspaper at the opposite end of the food establishment. On a good day, Chloe would have swooned over how beautiful and breathtaking this place was. But today was not a good day now. Was it?

She was trying to make out what happened overnight, but her brain couldn't comprehend it. Or maybe her brain didn't want to acknowledge what happened. How could William break up with her over something that? Chloe tried hard to think of something she might have said to offend him, but nothing came to mind.

She let out a ragged breath and blew it into her hands. Her hands wouldn't stop shaking no matter how she tried to steady them. Her friends would likely walk into the restaurant anytime soon, and she didn't want them to see her like this.

Today they were celebrating Ava. A week ago, they found out

that she was pregnant, and Mia had suggested that they have a little get-together at this expensive restaurant to celebrate the soon-to-be mother. If it wasn't for Ava, Chloe would have stayed home under her covers, crying her heart out.

How could she not have known? Chloe thought sadly. She wasn't the type of person who got a happy ending. All the men she had met in her life had either lied, cheated, or have left her, but when she met Sergeant Henley William, she had told herself to push aside her doubts, and before she knew what was happening, she was in love with a man who made her forget every single heartbreak. He made every hurt she had ever felt feel like a distant memory.

What was she supposed to do now when the person she placed her entire trust in betrayed her as if it were nothing! A tear fell down her cheek, despite her best efforts to hold back the tears. She quickly ran her hands gently over her face to dry her tears while trying not to smear her makeup.

The voices coming from the entrance made her turn to find all her friends walking toward her, and suddenly she found herself smiling when she saw Ava walking like she had carried dumbbells all day. Chloe chuckled and picked up her phone to check the time. She was going to reprimand every single one of them for being late.

A small shriek escaped her lips when she saw her reflection on her phone screen. If her friends saw her swollen eyes and smeared mascara, she wouldn't be able to hide anything from them.

Chloe dipped her hand into her bag and brought out her make-up purse. She sprang to her feet and dashed toward the ladies' room before her friends could reach her.

Once inside the bathroom, she quickly applied the magical touch to her face. She started by rubbing off the mascara with her wipes; then, she retouched her face with some foundation and concealer. Chloe forced a smile that didn't reach her eyes, but it had to be enough. She was the queen of faking the things she didn't feel. She just had to get through today without breaking down for Ava's sake, and after today's gathering, she could crawl back into her bed and cry to her heart's content.

There was a soft knock on the door. "Are you OK in there?"

Chloe heard Avery's concerned voice and bile rose in her throat as the tears threatened to start all over again. "Yes. Give me a minute. I will be out in a second," Chloe said quickly.

Avery laughed. "A minute or a second, which is it? Make up your mind, would you."

"You are funny." Chloe chuckled despite herself.

She opened the door to find Avery smiling cheekily from ear to ear. There was something about her smile that made Chloe's heart ache once more, and before she knew it, her arms were around Avery's neck, giving her a bone-crushing hug.

Avery gasped. "Hmm…You know I love you, right? And I know that I don't have a man and all…but I am not into girls. I promise you."

Chloe chuckled softly, pulling out of Avery's embrace. "You look good, Avery," she said, complimenting her petite friend's sense of style.

Avery made a small twirl. "What can I say? I have a model for a friend."

Chloe laughed again, much too loudly that Avery was taken aback.

"Are you okay, girl?"

Chloe nodded. "Of course, I am. Let's go see the new mother-to-be."

"Wait."

"What happened?" Chloe asked, hearing the concern in Avery's voice.

"Ava isn't pregnant."

Chloe blinked, baffled. "Uh?"

"She found out she had an ectopic pregnancy. She 'isn't pregnant."

"Why didn't anybody think to tell me anything. Am I not her friend. What if I had said something that could have hurt her feelings?" Chloe was angry, concerned, and overwhelmed.

"She wanted to tell everyone herself. You looked very excited about the baby, that's why I told you. I am sorry. I didn't mean to hide anything from you."

Chloe sighed. She couldn't imagine how Ava felt right now. Tears threatened to fall once more, but she threw her head back, opened her mouth, and fanned her face with her palms. She shook her head with more resilience.

Today is still about Ava; Chloe cautioned herself mentally.

"Let's go out; we can't say here all day." Chloe smiled broadly.

"I don't know if it's about Ava or something else, but you are acting weird."

Chloe waved her hand in the hair. "Of course, detective. You are free to continue seeing things that are not there."

Avery felt like talking, but she tightened her lips shut and walked ahead while Chloe followed closely behind. As soon as Chloe got back to the main restaurant, she threw her hands around her friends one by one, glad to see them.

"I have missed all of you," she crooned against their necks.

Minutes later, after their food had been served, Ava picked up a wine glass and said, "So, I had an ectopic pregnancy." She smiled softly, trying to downplay the way she felt. "I don't know how I can love something that I never had. But I do, and it is gone"

Ava's voice broke, but the petite woman squared her shoulders and smiled. "Antonio has been a God sent, and we have been holding it together."

Her four friends looked at her with pain in their eyes. They wanted to comfort their best friend, but they also knew Ava needed time to heal, and crowding her with their emotions would do more harm than good.

"I am sorry for your loss." Chloe stretched her hand and cupped Ava's hand in hers.

Mia looked confused. "So, why didn't you tell any of us? We could have been there for you." Her Texas drawl was more pronounced because of her emotions.

Avery gently tapped Mia on the shoulder, but she shrugged her off. Mia knew that Ava was hurting, but she was angrier at the fact that Ava didn't think they should know about her pain.

"I am sorry, Mia. I found out the pregnancy was ectopic two weeks ago."

"Two weeks ago?" Avery almost shouted, standing up with a startled expression. "You told me a week ago!"

Ava laughed nervously. "Em… em…"

"What are you hiding from us? You are acting weirder than usual," Olivia, who had been staring at the whole drama in front of her, quietly quipped.

"No, I'm not acting weird. Nothing is weird." Ava shrugged her shoulders but didn't make contact with any of her girls.

"Spill it. Now," Mia ordered unapologetically.

"This is not my fault." Ava threw her hands in the air. "Come out now, William. They will eat me alive if you don't!"

"William?" Chloe asked, turning around to look at her surroundings but didn't see anyone. "What are you-"

The sound of African drums filled the air as a highly decorated trolley carrying a cake was rolled toward the girls. All the women, except Ava, glanced at one another in surprise. The room was suddenly dimly lit, and on the walls of the restaurant, the words "Will you marry me?" were projected on it.

"Did Ivan prepare this?" Mia whispered to Olivia.

"How would I know? And Ava is already married."

"So, who could it be? …some other guests?" Olivia asked again.

They didn't have to wait long, as a man playing guitar walked in, and to everyone's surprise, it was none other than William.

"You?" Chloe shot out of her seat in shock.

William smiled and went down on one knee in front of Chloe. He opened a ring box while beaming from ear to ear. "So, will you marry me?" he asked, breathing heavily.

Chloe was dumbfounded. Wait, what was happening? William had broken their engagement last night. "But…we…I"

Her friends cooed at the beautiful sight in front of them. No one had expected this. Maybe Ava had known about it, but the other girls were short of words.

"So, do you?" William asked again.

"Yes!"   her friends shouted enthusiastically.

Chloe shook her head and softly said, "No!"

The African drummer stopped drumming, and then everyone went silent. That was not the answer everyone was expecting.

"What? Why..." William asked, his face white with shock.

Chloe picked up her bag and started heading for the door. Mia ran after her and grabbed her hand before she could open the door.

"What are you doing? This is a man you are already engaged to?"

"He...he broke up with me already!" Chloe shouted. "For no reason. He broke up with me!"

Mia, Olivia, and Avery turned around to glare at William, who quickly waved his hands in defense. Ava, in a corner, opened her mouth in shock, but no one was looking at her.

"That's not what happened...no, I mean that is what happened," he stuttered, trying to find the right words. "I was trying to surprise you! I would never intentionally hurt you."

"Let me get this right. You broke up with Chloe to surprise her?" Olivia asked, glaring at William like a kid caught with his hands in the cookie jar.

"Yes... I mean..." He closed his mouth.

"So you hurt my friend because you wanted to propose to her?" Avery asked, baffled.

"I mean, yes. No. I mean, No!" William looked like he put his feet in his mouth every time he tried to speak, so instead of trying to convince Chloe's friends, he wanted to explain himself to his woman. "Babe, you know that I would never try to hurt you."

"It was my idea!"

Everyone turned to face the person who said those four words. It was Ava, on her kneel, holding her ears, looking like she would rather be anywhere else.

"What?" Chloe asked in disbelief.

"Two weeks ago, William came to meet me. He wanted to surprise you. Re-proposes to you, you know. He felt he didn't do it right the first time..." Ava said, avoiding her friend's gaze. "He wanted me to help plan a surprise for you, and this was also around the time I found out about the ectopic pregnancy. So, I suggested that I would keep the pregnancy a secret not to dampen the

surprise and also because I didn't want to make a big deal out of it"
A tear fell down Ava's face despite her trying to hide her pain.

Ava walked slowly towards Chloe and held her gently by the shoulder. "I know how this looks like, but I really wanted to forget my pain, and William understood, so when I focused on the surprise plans. I forgot all about the pains I felt."

All the girls wrapped their hands around Ava and cried. They cried, feeling bad that Ava had hidden her hurt all this while because she was trying to make one of them happy. Ava scoffed; she hadn't known how much she truly needed her girls until she felt their warm arms around her. She sighed, chuckled, and used her hand to raise Chloe's teary face-up.

"It was my idea, so blame me. Not him; he loves you so much that he asked a dumb ass bitch like me for advice. I suggested the break up because you would be surprised when he proposed after, and to be honest, William said it was a bad idea, but I...I don't know what I was thinking," Ava said, stumbling through all the words at the same time.

Everyone gasped in shock at Ava, while Chloe ran back to meet William, who was still on his knees looking lost. She wrapped her arms around him, almost choking him, but he didn't care. He was glad that she had forgiven him.

"So, is that a yes?" Ava asked, her voice almost a whisper.

Mia, Olivia, and Avery tried to hide the laughter threatening to overpower their senses. They couldn't, in their wildest dreams, have assumed that Ava could pull off a stunt like the one she pulled.

William pulled back gently to stare at Chloe's tear-stained face. He used his fingers to wipe off the tears while she hiccupped.

"I am so sorry," he said.

She hit him gently on the shoulder. "Don't you ever try that again? Like ever!"

William chuckled but nodded like a child. "I won't; I cross my heart and...."

"Shh," Chloe put her finger on his lips, "don't say stuff like that."

"So, will you marry me?"

Chloe nodded shyly and buried her face in his neck. William smiled; instead, he beamed like a star. "That is not an answer. Is it a yes or a no?" he asked again.

"You know I meant yes," she said, still covering her face.

Everyone laughed at Chloe, seeing as she was acting like a lovestruck schoolgirl was the best thing ever.

CHAPTER TWO

William was on his way to pick her Chloe. He had called a few seconds ago and told her that he was almost there. She left her bedroom, closing the door gently behind her. She walked to the front door when she heard a car door lock. She could spot him on her porch, raising his balled fist to knock on her door. She hurried toward the door and opened it before he could knock.

"Hey." She rushed over to hug him, relishing in the feeling of his arms around her slim waist.

"Hello, Gem." He kissed her hair, breathing in her scent. "You look so beautiful tonight."

He did too. He was dressed in a white shirt with the sleeves neatly rolled up his forearms and black suit pants. From the looks of it, he wanted to pull off the casual look, and he did. His blonde hair was curled at the sides, with a few tendrils left to frame his chiseled face. He was nothing like the soldier she fell all over at the airport. He was here, in her apartment, looking like a regular guy. Her regular guy.

He led her to the limousine parked on the street. She slid in while the driver, a tall man dressed in a tuxedo and with the brightest smile, held the car door for them.

A sense of hope and longing crept over her as the car pulled away from the curb.

With her left fingers loosely in his, he played with them, her head beneath his chin.

"I love your shampoo. What's in it?" he queried, sniffing her hair, realizing that it was different from the scent he was accustomed to.

" Lavender and black wood," she replied, "I decided to switch since I love the smell of the wood."

" I do, too; it's relaxing."

The driver asked if they wanted music. He looked at her, wordlessly asking for her opinion. She nodded and said, "Something soothing will do."

"Oasis" by Sam Smith blasted through the car radio. "I love this song," William said, humming the lyrics under his breath.

She tipped her face up and kissed him on the lips. "I love you," she whispered, her eyes glued to his.

"I love you, Chloe," he replied as he pulled her into his lap and held her tightly to his body.

She leaned her head against his chest, his heartbeat ringing in her ears. She draped her hands around his neck and pulled his face to rest on her shoulder.

"How was your day?" she asked quietly.

"It was long and drab. Things heated up when my team and I had to rescue this young boy from drowning. His family was on their way to Mississippi."

"Oh my God."

"Yeah. I'm glad we saw him before he got taken by the tide." He rubbed circles into her back. It was nothing sexual, just soothing. She almost drifted off to sleep, but Sam's voice forced her to open her eyes.

"We're here, Sir, Ma'am," the driver announced. He parked in front of the blue and white building and then opened the door. William stepped down first, then held his hand out to her.

"Thank you." She smiled.

William whispered something to the driver before turning to lead her into the building. There was a lady at the door, and she cracked a wide smile the moment she saw them. "Hello, welcome to Rico's. Do you have a reservation, please?" she asked, opening her notepad.

"Yes," Chloe said and mentioned her name.

She smiled and nodded. "Follow me, please."

She took them to a long table with super comfortable red leather seats. "Someone will be with you soon," she said, then walked back to the door.

"You look amazing tonight, Darling." He reached out to hold her hand across the table, weaving his long, slim fingers around her dainty ones.

Chloe's smile warmed considerably. "Thank you, Will."

A waitress came over to them. She looked twenty-ish with dimpled cheeks. She asked them what they'd like to drink then dropped two menus on the table. "I'll come back for your orders." She paused and stared between them, trying to decide who to ask first. Her eyes settled on Chloe.

"Can I get you anything to drink? Water, wine, juice?"

"Water will be fine," Chloe said.

She looked over at William. "Same with the lady, please," he told her.

"This place is fine. I love the view from here," William commented, looking around the restaurant. The place was filled with couples and families having dinner. The kids were well behaved. There was no one running around, chasing the lights or something that caught their eyes.

"Rico is doing a nice job," Chloe said, complementing the owner of the restaurant.

His gaze landed on her, her cheeks glowing under the lights. He wanted to take her in his arms and kiss her senselessly. Then, she smiled, her eyes glossing over with what he couldn't decipher. He lifted her right hand and kissed her palm. "Want to talk first or eat?" he queried, his lips pausing over her palm.

"Eat. I'm starving," she replied without hesitation, turning rosy red.

"Me too," he returned, gently setting her hand down on the table. The air buzzed around them, making him sweaty even under the air conditioner, his gaze intent on her face until she looked away, picking up the menu.

His response made her wonder if he was referring to food. She was not. She wanted him to bury himself inside of her and take her to the edge over and over again. But Chloe remembered how William had promised when they were in Rio that they wouldn't have sex again until they got married so that Chloe could see that he loved her and not just the love-making part.

Rico spotted them from across the room and came over to say hello. "I'm glad to have you here again," his voice rang behind them.

" Oh, hey, Rico," Chloe greeted him, smiling brightly.

"How's Mia?" he asked as soon as he reached their table.

Chloe bit her lips, unsure of what to say. "She's fine." She wanted to ask him if he knew that Mia had a huge crush on him, but Chloe shook her head. There was no need to stir the hornet's nest if he didn't.

"Would you like to order now, Sir, Ma'am?" Rico asked.

William looked at the menu again. "I'll go for *bren en croute* and spinach tattles," he read off the menu.

The waiter looked over at Chloe. "Ma'am?"

"Wild Alaskan salmon," she said, "and some red grapes, please."

The waiter nodded and went off to prepare their order. Rico, who had moved to the next table to talk to the kids, returned to their table. "Please, if you need anything, let me know. I'll be happy to attend to you." He waved at them and walked back into his office, which was at the side of the restaurant. Chloe had been in there once when she wanted to order takeout for the girls, and she needed his input on the right food choice to get. Rico wasn't just an ordinary restaurant owner; he was an expert on food and wine. He knew the perfect weather to enjoy a particular drink and the best wine to accompany a plate of food.

Her phone vibrated in her purse; she glanced at him, silently asking if it was okay to check her messages. "It's probably the girls checking in," she said when he nodded.

It was. They were asking her a series of questions in the group chat. Avery was sending all kinds of emojis to her phone.

"Still at Rico's," she texted back, with an eye-roll emoji.

"Everything okay?" William asked

"Yea." She dropped the phone back into her purse then picked up her water glass.

The food arrived then, followed by a second person carrying a bottle of wine in an ice bucket.

"Rico said this will go well with the food," the young lady said, placing it in the center of the table.

"Thank you," William said, smiling politely at her.

They ate in silence, with William glancing over at her once in a while like he was making sure she was okay and enjoying her meal. She could feel his eyes on her but refused to look up.

William had never experienced an attraction so pure...so beautiful. So easy... She made him want to undo the things he did in his life before her and start all over on a clean slate. She was beautiful with flawless skin, and her face was bare of makeup except for mascara, highlighting her big brown eyes, making them appear bolder and prettier. His eyes moved to her lips; they were soft-looking and wet from the wine she had just sipped. She licked the droplets off her lips, swiveling her tongue once...twice over it. Her eyes were glued to her food, which was half-finished. He knew she could feel the heat that was buzzing around them. He couldn't be alone. It was too powerful, too raw to go unnoticed.

She glanced up when a waiter came to refill their wine glasses. "Thank you," she said, her voice inaudible, even in the almost quiet setting.

He kicked her leg gently under the table, trying to make her look at him. Her blush deepened. Resigned, she looked up at him and crinkled her forehead dramatically. "You should finish your food, Will. We have so much to talk about tonight." She moved her head sideways, her silver earrings catching the lights.

"We could talk some other time," he started, his voice low and husky, "I just want to look at you tonight and talk about nothing." He winked at her, making her laugh. The sound rumbled in her chest as she reached across the table to hold his hand.

"Okay, but we need to," she said, knotting his fingers with hers, "can I at least tell you where I want us to have our wedding?"

He couldn't deny her that, even if he wanted to. Her eyes twinkled with delight, and he was eager to hear where she'd chosen, so he nodded. "Please. I know I'm going to love it."

She exhaled, her lips slightly parted. "Um, Jamaica." She watched his face closely, seeking a reaction. She couldn't decipher the slight frown he sported for a nanosecond. She expected him to withdraw his hands, but he didn't. He held on tighter, his knuckles turning white.

She poured more wine into his glass and pushed it toward him. "Drink," she told him, and he took a long sip, letting the liquid burn his throat. He pushed the glass away and reclaimed her hand.

"My parents were on their way to our holiday villa there when their plane crashed. They died only the spot, along with my only sibling, Rebecca."

She gasped, her eyes misty. "I'm so sorry, Will. I had no idea." She went over to hug him, pulling him into her arms. "I'm so sorry," she repeatedly said, sobbing into his shoulder. He wrapped his arms around her and kissed her hard. Not minding the others around them. He needed to embed himself in her; he needed some of the light she was carrying. She made him feel alive, loved, and utterly cherished.

They didn't hear their plates bring cleared away and a note being dropped on the table. They didn't even take notice of the light in their part of the room being dimmed, giving away only their silhouette.

He sniffed, trying to keep the tears at bay. Each time he remembered his parents, his chest tightened, and he felt the pain of losing them all over again. The hurt was different, and he always ended up with a migraine or worse. But this time, it was different. He felt lighter talking about it with her. He would tell her everything, and maybe, she'd help him heal.

"Want to talk here or in the car?" Chloe asked, sensing his need.

"In the car," he said. "But let me settle the bill first."

He noticed the note then; it was folded in twice. He opened it and read, "Rico said he'll add it to my tab." He dropped a huge tip. Rising, he pulled her up with him then walked out of the building, his steps slow and heavy. She felt terrible for bringing it up as the glint she saw in his eyes earlier was no longer there. She was going to make this better. Help him keep their memory and talk about them without hurting so much.

The limousine was parked at the same spot they had left it. She had thought the man had left or something. He came around to open their door. "Did you have a nice evening, Miss Chloe?" he asked, bowing slightly. She replied in the affirmative, then scanned the darkened interior, struggling to make out things in the car. William entered behind her; then, the man closed the door softly.

"Where to, Sir?" he asked, putting the car in reverse.

"Drive around the block, Sam." The New York City lights looked beautiful as he peered through the window, admiring the Broadway and the Empire State Building. Sam drove slowly, the soft music playing silently from the car radio. When they drew closer to Midtown Manhattan, Sam asked if they wanted to take a stroll.

"No, but you can if you want," William had answered.

Sam parked the car in a reserved spot for cars under the bridge. The moment he was gone, William pulled Chloe closer and kissed her hard on the lips, his tongue probing, seeking for entrance. She obliged, swiveling her tongue around his, her hands placed on his hard chest. He moaned into her mouth, the sound making her pull him closer. "Hmm," she hummed, drawing away from the kiss.

He placed his forehead on hers and breathed into her mouth, his minty scent warming her face.

"Want to tell me about what happened?" she whispered, even though they were alone.

He nodded, then moved his head away, "It happened during my finals," he started, his voice barely audible that she had to lean on his chest to hear him properly.

"I was supposed to join, but exams were starting the following day, so we decided I'd join them as soon as I finished my last paper." He sucked in a breath. His voice sounded sad; he was frustrated with the cards life had dealt him

She took his hands in hers and wrapped them around her waist.

"Continue, please."

"I saw the news of their death on the news. I wasn't contacted. Everyone thought I had gone with them because I was always kinda invisible in school. The quiet nerd with headphones and glasses." He gave a dry laugh and wiped his face with his sweaty palm.

Recognition flickered in her eyes. "I saw the news. I was supposed to be on that plane too, but I was down with the flu. I had to reschedule."

His chest shook then, with heart-wracking sobs. She massaged his back gently, whispering words she couldn't even make out into his ears. She willed her tears to not flow, as one of them needed to stay strong.

His laughter rang in her ears, and she paused the movement of her hands and raised his head from her shoulder. "What's funny, Sir?" She asked with a quizzical look.

He continued laughing, then tucked her hair behind her ear. "You said 'fish salad and baked beans' three times." She frowned slightly, trying to remember when she even mentioned beans.

"Now you're making things up, William Henley," she said, feigning annoyance.

"No, I'm not, Babe. That's what you said into my ear.," he said with laughter in his voice. She hugged him tighter, thankful that he was out of that funk. No one deserves something that terrible.

"I'm glad you didn't get on that plane, or else I would have lost you too," he said.

"You wouldn't have," she replied. At his puzzled look, she continued. "Because we didn't know each other then."

"Hmm, but I wouldn't have met you," he argued. She rolled her eyes. He was trying to ignite an argument from her, so they'd make out afterward. But she was scolding herself for not knowing this part of him after they had been together for a year.

"I'm sorry, Will," she whispered into his hair, then bent her head to kiss him. "I'm sorry I didn't ask you sooner," she murmured, "I thought the Andersons were your parents."

He shook his head that was resting on her temple. "No, they're

Craig's. He's outside the State."

"Craig, your best friend?"

" Yes."

A heaviness settled in her chest, spreading through her whole body, and for a moment, she couldn't move but held onto him like she didn't want him ever to go away. He snuggled into her body, basking in the warmth that emitted from her. She glanced over at the brightly lit streets; she could see a couple kissing under the bridge, a bit farther from where they were parked, some girls throwing a softball and laughing, the sounds echoing through the streets.

"Tell me about your parents and Rebecca," she said.

He did, his voice quiet and sad. She felt bad for making him recount it. But he'd kept it all bottled for so long.

"We had plans, you know, to travel the world, see as much as we can," he was saying. She held onto him, encouraging him to go on. She closed her eyes, focusing her mind on his words. She wanted to remember them too, the people that birthed the man that had shown her that there was more to life. He may not have noticed the impact he had on her life, but she certainly could.

"Just so you know," he started, dragging his hand slowly through her hair, "life without them was a lonely place. It was both scary and tough. It was draining. Things got better after I met you. The thought of you in my life pulls me through each day, Chloe."

They stayed interwoven for an hour, letting the silence wrap around them like a soft blanket.

A rap at the window startled them. "You need anything, Sir, Ma'am?" Sam asked, his voice muffled through the glass.

"No, Sam," Chloe said, pulling away from the warmth of his arms, but her hands still entangled in his hair.

"Let's take Chloe home, Sam," William said.

Sam nodded, waved goodbye to his new friends, and got into the car.

As they drove across town, the roads were a tad deserted, as people were likely at parties since it was a Friday night. She had shifted onto the space beside him, but her head was in his arms. She looked at him sideways, trying to decipher his mood. The hard edges had loosened a bit, the colors returning to his face. She leaned up and kissed him.

"What was that for?" he asked, holding her face in his right palm.

"That was me saying thank you for being amazing. I love you, Will," she whispered.

Sam parked in front of the tall brick building that had been her home for the past few years. He wanted to come down to open the car door for her, but William stopped him. "I'll do it, Sam. I need to walk her in anyways" he turned to her, "milady." She batted his hands away and gingerly stepped out of the car.

Her apartment was on the ground floor. She took her keys from her purse and inserted them into the lock. "Want to come in?" she asked him, pushing the door open.

"What are you offering?" He tilted his head to the side, a playful glint in his eyes.

"Coffee? Tea?" she giggled.

"No, you?" He stepped toward her, pushed her into the house, and closed the door with a soft bang. "Don't be selfish, Chloe, kiss me."

She did, with her arms wrapped around his neck. Her breasts pressed against his chest. He whimpered into her mouth, sucking gently on her upper lips.

"I feel like taking you right now, against this door," he cooed in her ears.

She giggled. "You can't do that, Will."

"But I want to," he purred.

She gave a light-hearted laugh. "Go home, Babe. I'll see you next week Friday." She pecked his forehead, then allowed her lips to linger for a minute longer. "Then think about where you want us to have our wedding," she added. He nodded, then bade her good-night.

She watched him walk away before closing the door and locking it.

Her phone beeped with a text; she ignored it. Probably the girls are checking if she'd gotten home. She threw the phone on the bed, undressed, and got into her nightshirt with panties. She went to the kitchen to get a glass of water then back to the room. Her phone beeped again. She picked it up, and it was a message from William. He was the first texter and had sent a follow-up when he didn't get a reply from the first message. She read the messages, typed in a response, and pressed send.

It was 11 pm when she settled into the soft blanket, drifting off to sleep soon afterward.

CHAPTER THREE

"**W**hose funeral, Felicia?" Chloe quipped.

Felicia laughed, then set the materials on the empty couch against the wall. "They're from Mrs. Preston. She asked that you select the one that would go with the theme for this year's Christmas party at the White House."

" But the theme hasn't been released yet, or have you heard anything?"

" No, Chloe," she replied. "I told her, but she said you should call the secretary and ask."

Chloe thanked her, then she picked up the office phone and dialed the secretary's number. After the third ring, the secretary answered the call. Chloe explained her dilemma to the secretary, who told her what Felicia had said earlier. A theme had not yet been selected.

Tired, she stood up and walked over to the miniature coffee maker in her office. It was a wonder how they were able to find a place for it, as the room was covered in clothes and a sewing machine for whenever she needed to make a quick repair on a dress for a client.

She sipped slowly from the cup, allowing the hot black liquid to flow down her throat.

Felicia popped her head through the half-opened door, saying, "There's a delivery here for you, Ma'am."

"Oh?" Chloe mused, trying to think of what it could be. She wasn't expecting any delivery.

When Chloe saw the card, she knew it was from William. His distinct feminine handwriting was his trademark. She chuckled, remembering the first time William did something like this. She had asked him who wrote on the card, in reply, William had picked up a paper and pen from her desk and proceeded to prove that he did. She had spent the whole day taunting him.

She proceeded to open the package and saw that there were chocolates and a white rose in the box. William always outdid himself. She blushed, looking at the package again. Quickly, she took a picture of herself taking a bite of the chocolate while sniffing the flower.

William called her immediately. "You shouldn't have done that." His voice was husky, sending a shiver down her spine.

"Done, what?" she drawled.

"Sent that picture."

"Why?"

"Don't play with me, Babe. You know what I'm talking about."

She laughed loudly, which made him sigh at the other end.

"If you continue, I'll break my promise and fuck you before our wedding night, Chloe," he cooed.

She was about to say something when she heard Linda's voice in the background. She was his assistant. William told her to give him a second. "So, dinner tonight at yours?" he asked with the batted breath, knowing what day Mondays were for her.

"I can't, Will. I have to go up to the White House and meet with the secretary."

" Okay," he exhaled loudly through his mouth, "send me more of those pictures," he said, then hung up, not wanting to hear her laugh at him for complaining about something and asking for more in the next breath.

She went back to creating designs on the papers scattered around her, trying to decide on which to use for her wedding. It was almost noon, and she was yet to come up with something. She sighed, then stood up and walked over to the window overlooking the street. Her shop was on the 3rd floor of the plaza building. They were about seven floors, and each was occupied by people selling textiles, accessories, car parts, and a cleaning Agency.

***

"What the devil took you so long to get here, Craig?" William bellowed at his best friend, who had just arrived from Chicago.

"Calm down, tiger, I tried reaching you to let you know that my flight was delayed, but it went straight to voicemail. Linda's too," Craig returned.

William scowled and gave him a disbelieving look. "You own the plane." He paused and picked up his tie, then handed it to Craig to help him fix it. "Who was she?" he asked, buttoning his shirt

Craig shrugged his broad shoulders, feigning ignorance. "It's a he, remember, I named it after your father," he replied with a straight face.

"Don't play smart with me, Craig or I'm going to..."

Craig laughed, cutting him off. "You shouldn't be threatening me, man. I'm trying to fix your tie. You know what that means, hmm?" he asked with a faux seriousness in his baritone voice. "And," he continued, "don't threaten me with 'I'll exclude you from my wedding plans.' That's cheap." He laughed again when the scowl on William's face deepened. "I have my plane, and I can fly it anywhere," he added with a smirk, then patted William's cheeks.

"Ass," William muttered under his breath, but loud enough for Craig to hear.

"Dick. I can't believe you're getting hitched before me," Craig intoned.

"I've always been the responsible one," William said, happy that he had a comeback this time. Craig was always hitting him and hitting hard. He turned on his heels and smiled wryly. "You shouldn't have dumped Lisa; she was good for you."

Craig scoffed, waving him away. "She was after my money, and you said so too."

William shrugged. "But you were broke, right?"

"She saw the potential in me," Craig said defensively.

"If you say so," William said in a singsong voice, trying to get a rise out of his best friend. God, he had missed him, and having him back here was relieving. He couldn't wait for him to meet Chloe and maybe, Mia too. He contemplated sending a quick text to Chloe to inform her about Craig's arrival as he walked into his wardrobe and removed the black tuxedo from the hanger, but he'd rather wait and let it be a surprise. Tonight was their annual dinner to celebrate the year's achievements as soldiers. He was picking her up from her house on his way to the Stafford Hotels, where the event was being hosted. She had mentioned Mia wanting to tag along, and he had no qualms with that. He liked Mia, and a part of him wanted her to meet Craig, and maybe, they'd stir up something that could lead to more. She was a firecracker, but knowing Craig, he was one with fire and loved being challenged by a woman with spunk and beauty. Mia was both fierce and beautiful. He was a tad sad when Craig's plane didn't arrive when it was supposed to, he was only consoled by the fact that they'd get to meet in Jamaica. Speaking of Jamaica, he smiled at the thought of Chloe being overly worried and protective of him when he recounted the deaths of his parents and only sibling.

He had stopped talking about them many years ago because of the excruciating ache he always felt deep in his heart. Most people didn't know he had no parents. They all assumed he was the Andersons' son and Craig's brother due to their close-knit. Chloe made it easier, talking about them with her, which made him realize how much he'd missed them. He visited their grave every month with flowers and an oil perfume for Rebecca. She would have been 25 by now and helping Chloe with the wedding planning. His mom would have loved Chloe. His dad too. His old man was easygoing and the smartest person he knew.

The housekeeper came in then to ask if he needed anything. Craig dismissed him. "I'll handle whatever he wants, Felix."

William turned when he heard Craig's footsteps coming up behind him.

"You still alive in there?" Craig asked in a mock whisper.

William ignored him, his eyes searching for the perfect shoe to go with the tuxedo. He settled for the brown lace-up croc.

"Have you told her yet?" Craig queried. He was standing at the door, with his right hand placed on the doorknob.

"No, I intend to tonight."

"Are you sure about this?" Craig pushed, arms crossed, as he leaned against the doorpost.

"Yes, Dad. Now stop treating me like a toddler and come help me fix this," he said, his tone almost angry.

Craig went over to him, helped fix his buttons, and then patted his back. "I'm just looking out for you, Champ."

Champ. That was the name they all called him - Craig and his parents. They believed in him so much. Even when he got Pamela pregnant, they stood by him and helped raise the boy until Pamela started acting like the spoilt bitch she was, which she, too, took him to notice when they first met. They got a place for her, and Rosie, Craig's mother, had been helping him check things out. Ensuring that his boy was fed and well looked after.

"Thank you, Craig," he said, hugging the other man.

"Anytime. Anytime, brother."

Sam was waiting for them outside with the Rolls Royce Dawn. It was William's latest addition to his fleet of cars. He had a thing for automobiles, loved buying them.

Sam bowed when he saw them approach. He was dressed in a tuxedo too, and his wristwatch was glittering under the light. William nodded at him and asked about his wife and two kids.

"They're very well, Sir," Sam replied, his smile broadening.

Craig trotted behind him, his eyes glued to his phone. He was smiling at something he was watching or reading.

"Come on, man. We're late," William called out to him. "Go on, Sam; he'll close the door. Thank you."

Craig slipped into the car, whistling under his tone.

"Happy about something?" William needled him.

"Yes," Craig droned, "I can't wait to see Chloe," he added.

"Me too," William mumbled.

Craig patted his hand that was closer to him. "I'm happy for you."

"Thank you."

The rest of the drive down to Chloe's house was made in silence, with just the sounds coming from the radio. A hip-hop song was on. Craig closed his eyes, nodding his head slowly to the beats.

The car stopped in front of the house. William could see the light coming from her bedroom, and he spotted her moving around in circles. Was she dancing? He chuckled at the thought, the sound waking Craig up from his catnap. He looked visibly tired; William almost pitied him.

He opened the door and slid out to get his woman. He knocked twice before the door was pulled open. Mia stood at the door dressed in a blue dinner dress with glitters at the sides and a lacey material covering her cleavages. William averted his eyes, looking at her red hair trimmed and curled at the top instead.

"She's almost ready and will be...." Mia started to say before he could ask, but she was cut off by the sounds of Chloe's heels on the tiled floor.

They both turned at the same time to the direction of the sound.

William's breathing ceased. He stared awestruck by the beauty that was engaged to be married to him in a few months.

Chloe smiled, proud at the effect she was having on him. Mia, who had noticed the air around them was getting mushy, slipped into the house and grabbed her bag. They were still in the exact position she had left them in when she came out. She chuckled and pushed past William without uttering a word, not wanting to disrupt whatever it was they were doing.

Chloe cleared her throat. "I love your shoes." *Really, Chloe,* she chided herself, resisting the urge to pull at her hair.

William smiled and walked toward her. "Thank you. You look and smell exquisite," he said, taking her in his arms. "Can I kiss you, or will I ruin your makeup?" he asked in a frisky tone. His eyes seeking hers.

"Damn the makeup, Will. Kiss me, please?"

He did. His tongue going right for hers. He wasn't slow this time but unhurried and possessive.

The car honked, causing them to break apart. She giggled. "Sam is sure getting impatient." she quipped.

"That's not Sam. It's Craig," at her arched eyebrow, he continued, "he came in today, and he wanted to surprise you, but I guess he's ruined it now."

He chuckled, his chest vibrating against hers. "Come on, let's go make him jealous," he drawled with a wink.

Craig had moved to the front seat and laughed at something Sam said. They were expecting to see Mia in the car, but she wasn't there. Chloe looked back to check if her car was still parked in the parking space, but it wasn't. Which meant the other girl had decided to drive herself to the party—typical of Mia.

"She's left in her car," Chloe said, then slid through the open door of the Rolls.

Not giving her time to settle in properly, Craig leaned over and hugged her. "It's so nice to meet you, Chloe, finally."

His forwardness didn't rattle Chloe. She leaned into him. "I've heard so much about you, Craig. It's nice of you to be here."

William rolled his eyes. "I need you, Babe. It's cold here."

Chloe and Craig separated. Craig turned to Sam. "Turn off the AC, Sam. Your boss is cold."

William smacked his head lightly. "Ouch!" He turned to glare at William. " What did you do that for?"

"It's hot in here; turn the AC back on," William said, snuggling closer to Chloe, then smirking at Craig.

"Ass," Craig muttered.

Craig and William ignored each other for the rest of the drive. Craig asked Chloe tons of questions just to get on William's nerves. Chloe played along, ignoring William too. Sam was chuckling, greatly entertained. On the other hand, William wore a scowl throughout the ride, his arms folded across his chest.

When they arrived at the hotel, Sam maneuvered the car into the space between a Ford GT and a Mercedes Benz. Craig applauded him, patting his hand and grinning widely.

William smiled too, nodding his head like a proud father. Sam opened the door. "Thank you, Sam," he held his hand out to Chloe, "come on, Babe." Craig snickered, which made Chloe giggle too, covering her mouth with the back of her palm.

"You look like someone stole your favorite shoe, Will. Something eating you up?" Chloe queried, baiting him.

He rolled his eyes dramatically and pulled her to him. "You just met him, and you're picking his side already. You hurt me really bad, Babe," he said, feigning hurt.

Chloe kissed his temple. "I love you, Will," she whispered.

The party was in full swing when they walked in. Chloe searched around for Mia and found her dancing with a dark-skinned man who was smiling down at her. And she was hoping to pair him up with Craig. She turned to William, whose eyes were also fixated on Mia. He was frowning slightly. She knew that he was planning the same thing with her at that moment.

"Go grab us a drink, Babe," she whispered in his ear. The music was too loud, and one could barely hear their thoughts. He nodded and walked off in the direction of the bar.

Craig had disappeared too, and Chloe didn't bother searching the crowd for him. She noticed a vacant table with two chairs and went over to sit there, watching out for William.

CHAPTER FOUR

Mia was bored, and she needed some air. She whispered something into the strange man's ears and pushed through the crowd toward the door, shunning his poor attempt at another dance. He wasn't even her type.

She noticed a back door that led to what looked like a garden and stepped through it. The cold wind blew against her skin. She packed her hair up as the breeze blew it all over her face.

She noticed a stairwell that led to a balcony. Wanting to be away from the buzz, she took it, thankful that her gown was knee length.

The place was empty. The couches were scattered with empty beer cans and pizza boxes stacked in a corner. It was ample space; there was no way she'd have to get close to the dirt pile. She stood against the railing, looking down at the soldiers and their dates trotting into the hall. She sighed, then leaned further into the rail.

"Hey, just calm down, and I'll get you some help," a voice said behind her. She ignored it, thinking he was on a call or reading a script.

The voice came again, this time closer and calmer like he was talking to someone that... wait, he probably thought she wanted to commit suicide. She laughed, then whirled around to face him. "Wait, you were talking to me," she said, not paying mind to his abs and muscles that were covered in a shirt a size smaller than him. The man knew he was hot as hell and was milking it.

Craig released a Long breath, running his palm down his face.

He was visibly shaken and pissed. She made a show of skipping off the step, and he was at her side before she could blink. "You okay?" he asked, holding her at arm's length to stare at her face. He examined her for injuries that were not there then his gaze landed on her lips. She chose that moment to swipe her tongue once over her lips, wetting them. He moved his face closer to hers; his eyes were dark and predatory.

She pushed away from him. "Thanks for looking out for me," she blurted, then turned on her heels, taking the steps two at a time, like she couldn't wait to get far away from him. Craig shook his head, trying to clear it. He put his hands on the rail, trying to see what got her so transfixed from that position. He Could see a couple kissing inside a car parked directly under the balcony. He looked away, his thought going back to the feel of her soft body in his arms. He exhaled slowly, struggling to blot out her intoxicating scent. *Was that magnolia?* He sniffed his hands, regretting not running after her.

Thank goodness she came alone. Mia didn't have to wait for a ride or go through the trouble of ordering a cab. She sent Chloe a quick test, informing her that she was heading home and not to worry about her. There was no car blocking hers, so she got in, turned on the ignition, and reversed out of the crowded parking lot.

She should have stayed home instead and read a book or stalked Rico on social media. Coming here was a waste of her time, or maybe it wasn't? She remembered the feel of his arms around her; it was rock hard and totally like that of a bestselling novel's male character. She didn't regret leaving though, men like that were only after one thing, and right now, she wasn't ready to be a man's plaything.

***

Chloe sipped the soda with a twist of lime as she charily looked around the packed dance floor for Mia. She couldn't spot Craig either. A tiny glimmer of hope sparked within her that maybe they had bumped into each other and were probably in a corner getting acquainted. She smiled into the drink, her mind already sketching Mia's wedding dress. She laughed out loud at the thought. To think that she could come up with a style for Mia that was yet to get a man. She felt an arm around her, snuggling into her neck. She leaned into him, thankful it was William and not one of the men going around and looking for women to snack on. She almost puked at the thought of a random drunk holding her. She'd hit his head with her 6 inches heels, smacking his brain into consciousness.

"Hey, Babe," she purred, kissing his earlobe.

"What were you smiling about?" William asked her.

" Um, nothing. Just trying to come up with designs for my wedding dress."

He took the empty seat beside her. "We can get something when we get to Jamaica, Babe. Don't stress it, okay."

Her heart stopped. Everything ceased at that moment. She screamed, but the loud music muffled it; only he could hear it. He opened his arms, and she sprung into them. Her eyes were glittering with unshed tears.

"Thank you, Babe," she breathed into his ears. "But are you sure about this?" she asked, searching his eyes for any hint of regret or sadness, but all she found there was an undiluted love, all for her.

She kissed him. "You don't have to answer; your eyes say it all."

He chuckled. "So you can read me now, huh?" he asked, his brows rising in mock wonder.

She nodded. "We've been together for more than a year now, Will. It would have been a huge failure on my part not to have the ability to read you," she cooed.

"Can you tell why I decided to have it there?"

She nodded, linking his fingers with hers. "You want to move on from the hurt," she started slowly like she was choosing her words carefully, "you want to see all the places you visited with them again." He grew silent, his eyes glued to hers. "And, you're doing this for me, knowing that I've always wanted to visit Jamaica," she concluded.

He beckoned to the server going around with a tray of drinks. He picked up one and handed it to her, then took another one for himself.

"You missed one thing," he uttered, his tone husky and sensual.

"What?" she asked.

"Why don't you try figuring this one out, smart ass," he chaffed.

"Don't turn this into a banter, William," Chloe deadpanned.

William lifted the wine glass and took a swallow. "Ah, this lot trying to get us drunk or what. What the hell is in this cup?" he asked no one in particular.

Chloe rolled her eyes and scoffed. "Chateau D'Yquem, and don't change the subject, William Jackson."

"You say that, so we'll. You're so smart, Babe," he purred.

He raised his palm in surrender when she gave him the stink eye. "Okay, slow down, tiger," he quipped, "I'll tell you."

William cleared his throat and drank the remaining wine in one gulp. "I want to make love to you on the beaches, walk butt naked and take tons of pictures."

She laughed. "With all those people that would be there?"

He shook his head. "We're going November and staying till mid-December; the crowd won't be extra," he said, looking at his phone.

She turned to see what he was looking at and found that he was on the internet, researching Jamaica. "Let me see that." She zoomed in on the picture. It was of a beach with the most transparent water she'd ever seen. The white sand and blue water drew her in. Then it struck her; she'd seen this before, in her dreams. But it was nothing close to these pictures, and she knew the real thing was going to be perfect. "What's this place." She zoomed out to check the name.

" Beaches Ocho Rios," he said, pointing out the name underneath the picture to her, "that's where we're going to stay if that's cool with you."

She danced in her seat; the move made the long slit on her Aggi black gown slip further up, showing off her tanned thighs and lacey thong. William sucked in a breath, willing his groin to stop pulsating. "It's cool, Babe." She hugged him, kissing him squarely on the lips. The bystanders oohed, clapping wildly at their show of affection. William chuckled, waving them off.

"Want to dance?" she asked, her voice throaty.

He looked at his crotch that was hard and pushing against the thick material of his trouser. "I can't, babe," he moaned.

"Come on, you can grind on my ass," she coaxed, holding his hand to make him stand up.

"How about you rub it for a while?"

Chloe's brow furrowed in faux horror. "Come on." She dragged him off the chair and led them to the face floor. It was dimly lit. *The uniform men sure do know how to have fun*, she mused. She felt his hand going up to her body till he got to her boobs. Her back was to him, and she could feel his hard member rubbing against her ass. She sighed. God knows if they continued this way, she was going to beg him to fuck her. Why the hell did they even make that pact in the first place, huh.

"When we get to the island, I'm going to marry you the next day, so we can spend the rest of our trip having mind-blowing sex at all the best places on the island," he breathed into her ears, moving slowly to the sensual song that the universe picked just for them.

"We will have to settle down first, Will. Scout out the best spot and get a clergyman to officiate the ceremony."

"Then we'll give it two days. No more, so don't ask."

"I'm not going to; I want to fuck you too. You drive me wild, Will," she purred, then moved her hips against him, gyrating on his front.

"Where the hell did you learn to do that?" he queried, his mouth agape. Fighting hard to conceal his frown.

"Parties? Internet? I don't know."

"Done this with anyone before now?" he asked, his voice laced with jealousy.

She laughed, turning to face him. "No, Babe. They didn't measure up." She turned her back to him and did it again. The slit pushed to the side; he ran his finger down her thighs, his fingers tethering at the edge of the thong. "Don't tease me, Will, I can't bear that," she pleaded, her voice raspy and her breath ragged.

He turned her in his arms, took a step back, and rotated his hips.

The crowd roared. He could hear Sam's voice egging him on with pride. He twirled her around, then bent his knee and rotated his hips again. Chloe laughed and spanked him. Then they bowed.

"You got moves, man," his superior said, patting his back. William smiled and thanked him.

The dance floor was cleared, and tables were arranged for the award and speech ceremony. William and Chloe took a seat by the left-hand corner. A server brought more drinks. William looked over at Sam to check if the young lad was drinking, but he was nursing a soda and talking with a lady that looked too young to be there.

The room grew silent as the Commandant read his speech.

"Is that your Commandant?" Chloe whispered.

"Yes."

"He's so old, man."

"That he is, but he's young at heart."

"Yeah, I figured. His voice is so vibrant," she said, then brought out her phone to take a picture of the man.

"I can send you the one I took together with him."

She nodded. "Thank you."

The rest of the evening was a blur until the Commandant announced that he had a special package for all the officers and their dates.

He instructed the servers to go around with the packages, wrapped in a blue sheet.

"Pick the one with your name on it," he said.

Everyone clapped and rose to thank him before he descended the stage.

When it got to William's seat, he found one with his name boldly inscribed and removed it, "Thank you," he said to the server.

He turned to Chloe and handed her the one marked "Date." She opened it. It was a bracelet, and underneath it was engraved the words 'you're beautiful.' It was a pure diamond.

"Wow, he sure went out of his way," she gushed.

"That's David for you, always topping the bar."

"What's in your box?"

He showed it to her. "It's a wristwatch with a tracker. It's something we've always wanted."

"Wow." She was awed by the man's generosity. Her father was like that too, always giving and expecting nothing in return.

The awards were handed out, and William was honored with the Best Team Lead of the Year. He wasn't surprised; he did give them his all and pushed his team to be the best.

After the closing remark, William in the company of Chloe went over to say hello to the Commandant.

The man was still very agile even in his early eighties. His British accent was thick. Several people came over to greet him, and he touched their hands and smiled as they passed.

He congratulated William on his award and commented on Chloe's dress. "That's the loveliest I've seen tonight," he whispered conspiratorially like he was sharing a huge secret with her. She laughed, her voice attracting others around them. They turned and stared at her, then the Commandant. Surprise registered on their faces.

"That's not true, Sir," she returned.

"It is. Come on, look at that," he pointed with his nose to a lady clad in a dress that was two sizes smaller than her. Her tits were popping out.

"Damn, that looks suffocating." Chloe laughed.

" I don't pity her at all," David added.

They spoke for a while about the army. David told her about his escapades and best death experiences. William stood to the side, watching them converse. He was stunned at the Commandant's easy banter with Chloe. That was a man that was never found in the company of women except for his wife and kids. He said women were trouble, and he'd had enough of them. But here he was, laughing with Chloe like he'd known her for years. His phone vibrated with a message. It was from Craig:

'Don't bother looking for me, Champ. And she's hot ASF.'

'What's her name?' He typed back.

'Don't know,' Craig replied.

'Red hair?' William asked.

'Nah, blonde.'

"Fuck!" William cursed under his breath. It wasn't Mia, so where the hell was she. He looked over at Chloe, and she was smiling widely. The Commandant patted her back fatherly and kissed her cheeks. David beckoned to William. "Congratulations, boy. Your lady here told me you're getting hitched this Christmas." His eyes were warm and proud.

"Thank you, Chief."

Chloe went over to him and pranced over to him for a kiss. "You, okay?" she asked, pulling him away from the little crowd that had started to gather around the Commandant

"Yeah. Can't find Mia, have any idea where she might be?"

She shook her head. "No, but I saw her across the room when we got here," she brought out her phone from her clutch, "let me call her." She unlocked the phone, and that was when Mia's text popped up on the screen.

"She left two hours ago," Chloe said, confusion written on her face.

"That means..." William started.

"She didn't stay for the party," Chloe cut in.

William nodded and showed him Craig's text. "He left too."

Chloe smiled. "That means..."

It was William's turn to interrupt her. "No, he said she's blonde."

"Fuck!" she cussed in a low voice.

William chuckled. "The same thing I said."

The dance floor was jam-packed again. The men had removed their tux and folded their shirts up to their arms. "Song two" was playing, and the ladies were grinding hard on the men. William spotted Steve, his youngest team member dancing with a man. It was a beautiful sight. William had always known the lad was gay when he was always ogling asses and blushing randomly.

"Wanna dance?" he asked Chloe.

"No, I need another drink. I'm heartbroken," she said with a dramatic scowl.

"Right away, milady," he bowed, "have anything in mind?"

"A cocktail should do."

He went off to the bar. She leaned against the table and un-locked her phone to send Mia a message, asking about her where-abouts. 'You okay,' she added after a second thought.

She checked her messages, replied to a few, and went back to Mia's. She found the dots moving, showing that Mia was typing a reply.

'Yours. Baking a chocolate cake, you in?'

Chocolate cake, Chloe checked the time. It was a minute past 10 pm.

'Yes, please. William too!' Chloe pressed send and tucked her phone back in her clutch when she noticed William approaching with her drink.

"Moscow mule." She smiled, taking a long sip.

William nodded. "You should open a bar, Babe," he added with a witty smile.

She nudged his arm. "It's the girls; we always make sure to ask questions at every bar we're visiting. Know what's in the drink and stuff like that."

They stood watching the crowd. Chloe smiled. These people deserved all the happiness in the world. She was happy they were getting it, thankful for the Commandant.   She sipped the cock-tail, letting the sour taste burn her throat before swallowing. She turned her gaze on William. She nudged him gently again. "We should head out, Will. Mia is alone at the house."

He nodded ."Give me a minute to go say hello to Steve." He trot-ted in the direction of the young man. Chloe watched as William patted the young man's back and shook his date's hand. With a final look at her man and the rest of the men, she drained her glass and then placed it carefully on the buffet table. There were no servers, so she figured it was a serve yourself kind of setting. She spotted a couple at the table next to her eating. She eyed the food, but she remembered Mia was making chocolate cake back home. She would pass, serve her belly for Mia's cake.

William returned to her side. "Let's go, milady," he held her hand, "the side exit is preferable at this point," he said, pulling her toward the left wing.

"Our coats," she told him.

"Sam has them."

The crowd was increasing. It looked like people came for the after-party.

Sam was spotted waiting in the hotel lobby for them. "This way, please," he said, leading them to where the car was parked. He opened the back door, and Chloe slid in first, then William.

"Thank you, Sam," William said.

Chloe noticed their coats hanging inside. She thanked him then relaxed into William's arms.

"Did you have fun?" William asked, resting his chin on her head. He could smell her lavender shampoo. He breathed in her scent, closing his eyes.

"Yes. I love David," Chloe said with a smile in her voice." He's funny and so easy to talk to."

William chuckled. "He's not. It's you, Chloe. You draw people in and make them feel safe like they can talk about anything with you."

She wanted to ask him why he didn't feel safe enough to tell her about his parents, but instead, she raised her head abruptly, hitting his face in the process. "Ouch," he let out, rubbing his jaw with his forefingers.

"I'm so sorry," she leaned in and kissed him, "I'm so sorry."

He bit her lips gently, then swiped his tongue over the spot. "It's fine, now I got to kiss you," he smirked, kissing her hair that was back under his chin.

She squinted. "So, David?"

"Yeah, he rarely speaks to women as he did with you," William said.

" Oh, he was cool, and I felt like we could talk forever, yunno."

William pulled her to sit on his lap. "You're like a magnet, Chloe. You attract people effortlessly."

She didn't say anything for a while; then, he put his head on her breasts. "Rest awhile, Babe. You've had a long day."

He snuggled in and closed his eyes. Maybe tonight, she'd let him pass the night at hers. It had been eons since he'd slept beside her.

Sam didn't turn on the radio; he figured the couple needed the silence. He drove slowly, navigating in and out of traffic with expertise.

Chloe's house wasn't far from the city tower. She loved the noise, so she had picked a spot closer to town. Sam stopped the car. He knew William wouldn't go home tonight, so he had driven onto the compound and parked in an empty spot. He'd leave the car there and get a cab home.

Chloe shook William awake then opened the door from her side as Sam handed the keys to her. "I'll come to pick him up in the morning," he said.

William told him not to bother. "I'll drive down myself, Sam. Go home; I'll see you next week."

The house was lit. Mia was lying face-up on the couch, watching a TV series. She looked up when she heard the front door opening. "Hey," she went over to hug Chloe first, then William, "how was the party?" she asked, taking Chloe's hand in hers and leading her to the couch while William trailed behind, unknotting his tie. He sat on the love seat, opposite Mia.

The girls were talking about the party. He just needed to shower and get into bed. So he excused himself and walked into Chloe's room.

"So, y'all ready to shag now?" Mia asked with a mischievous wink.

Chloe smacked her thighs. "No, he's just too tired, and I need him around to be sure he's okay."

Mia laughed. "You're lying. I've seen the way you eat him up with your eyes, Babe." She took a sip of the lemonade in a glass on the table. "I don't know why you are holding out, though," she added as an afterthought.

Chloe sighed, stretching her legs. Mia noticed that she was still wearing her heels and bent down to take them off.

"It was his idea. Something about wanting to do things right. Start things the right way," Chloe said, her expression sober.

Mia snorted. "Total waste of time if you ask m." She stood up from the couch, picking up the almost empty glass. "Go freshen up and come eat. I'll serve you the cake."

The room was dark except for the light streaming in from her bathroom door left ajar. William was sprawled face down on her giant sleigh bed; the covers pushed to the side. He had changed into one of her shirts and the boxers he left in her underwear drawer for times like this. His clothes were neatly folded and placed on the single couch in the right-hand corner of her room. She went over to the bed and sat down quietly beside him. He stirred but didn't open his eyes. "Go shower, Babe, and come to bed," he said drowsily.

"Okay," she said, then leaned down and kissed him before undressing and walking into the bathroom.

The water was warm against her skin as she stood under the big sprays from the showerhead. She closed her eyes, enjoying the feel of the water on her skin. She thought about David. He reminded her of her father tonight, who would have been 78 this year. She sighed, then picked up the shower gel and poured a little into her palm, then rubbed it on her face, scrubbing gently. She made a mental note to call her mother and tell her about her plans to marry outside the country and apologize. She knew her mother would be mad at her, as she was big on ceremonies and planning. After all, Chloe was her only child.

She kneaded her arms, searching for kinks to loosen. She picked up the sponge and poured a handful of gel on it, then scrubbed her back, belly, then lower. She rinsed the soap off. Her hair was spared, as she didn't want to go through the stress of drying it before bed.

She stepped out of the bathroom, closed the door gently behind her, and went over to the ornate dresser that was opposite the bed to apply her deodorant. She walked around the room, avoiding the parts of the floor that creaked to avoid waking William.

She got dressed in her nightie, a blue cotton gown that stopped mid-thigh, and walked stealthily out the door.

Mia was still on the couch, and a plate with chocolate cake was on the table with a glass of apple juice. "Thank you," Chloe said to her before taking a huge bite of the cake. "Hmm, this is good," she moaned, chewing slowly, then sipping the apple juice to wash it down.

"Why did you leave so early, Mia?" Chloe asked after swallowing the second bite.

"I wasn't enjoying it," Mia lied. She wasn't ready to meet anyone yet, and tonight had seemed like the men were too much, and there was no way she could have resisted the last one at the balcony. She just had to leave.

"Met anyone interesting?" Chloe asked.

Mia shook her head vehemently. "I just had a glass of expensive wine, then left."

"Why?"

Mia chuckled. "Stop with the questions, Chloe. I just needed to be alone and catch this program while I'm at it."

"I see that," Chloe said with a scowl, folding. "This is good, though. I'll save some for Will in the morning."

"Don't worry, I made enough, for Sam too."

"Thank you, Mia," Chloe said and hugged her side.

They sat in silence for a while. Mia was engrossed in the Tyler Perry movie she was watching and Chloe finishing up her meal. She stood up and took the plates to the kitchen, rinsed them, and put them in the dishwasher.

She poured herself another glass of juice and went out to the sitting room.

"Hey, do you think it's too late to call Mom?" Chloe asked, sitting back beside Mia.

Mia looked up from the TV. "Karen, hell no. She's probably up watching some crappy show on that TV of hers."

Chloe laughed. "You both belong together." Mia looked at her, her face folded in a thoughtful scowl, making Chloe laugh aloud. "Calm down. I'm talking about 'the crappy show' part." She made the quote and unquote sign.

"You're just boring. Tyler Perry is a joy giver. Come on, watch how this 'Sistas' movie is just...."

" Save it, Babe. I'd rather watch a cartoon than watch a bunch of grown ladies fights over a man," Chloe cut in with a wave of her hand.

"They're not fighting over a man; they're just..." Mia started defensively, but Chloe told her to save it again, then walked off into the kitchen to call her mom. Karen picked up after the third ring. "Hello, mother," she said into the phone. She could hear shuffling sounds. Her mother was probably sitting up from the couch where she was lying down to watch crappy series on the television.

"Nice of you to finally call your old woman, Chloe." Karen's voice was sharp, piercing through the phone.

"Mom, you know I've been swamped," she sighed, "And what stopped you from calling me?" she added as an afterthought.

Karen laughed. "I was busy too," she said, still laughing.

"Yeah, right, watching Tyler Perry, I guess."

"Among other things," Karen said suggestively.

Chloe stood up straighter. "You seeing someone, Mom?"

"No, I can never do that to your Pa." Chloe sighed again. She wanted her mother to go on dates and have fun, but Karen preferred sticking with the old ladies of Sunny Valley. It was a small community, where everyone knew everyone, so her mother was never lonely. But still, having a man to snuggle up to was bliss, and she needed that for her mother. "He would have done the same," Karen was saying.

Chloe couldn't dispute that. Her father wouldn't have remarried too, but how about an affair?

"How about an affair, Mom, maybe a man friend that could help mow the lawn and split the wood during the winter season?"

Karen ignored her daughter. "Mom?" Chloe called, removing the phone from her ear to check the signal. "Come on, Mother, I'm Just looking out for you," she continued.

"I can't believe you call me this late to talk about my dating life."

" Non- existing dating life," Chloe cut in.

"Whatever," Karen hissed in a breath and continued like Chloe didn't interrupt her. " We should be talking about your wedding to that god."

Chloe laughed at the last part. "Stop calling him that, Mom."

"He is. I was so proud the day he came by the house to say hello.

The old folks were Just oohing and aahing." She laughed, remembering how the old ladies kept touching him and gushing at his clear dark skin. "I can't wait to see you both get married," Karen added

" I know, Mom, but it's..."

" It can be in the garden you and your Pa started or the beach. What do you think, Chloe?"

God, this was going to be more complicated than she thought. "Mother," she drawled, "I'm not going to have the wedding here," she added with the batted breath, preparing herself for the onslaught of her mom's wrath. It came in the form of a piercing shriek that dared to destroy her eardrums. She removed the phone from her ear, dropped it on the counter, and put it on speakerphone.

"Stella and I already bought our dresses and fixed a date with the makeup artist. Take it back, Chloe; you can't do this to your Momma!"

Chloe walked over to the sink and grabbed a glass from the rack to fetch water and drink.

"Your Pa would have wanted you to have it here, in YOUR garden!" Karen was raging, her voice bellowing throughout the kitchen.

She opened the fridge and took out an apple. It was chill, and as she sank her teeth into it, the cold bit her teeth, making her wince.

"Was it his idea?"

Chloe chewed, swallowed, and bit into it again, taking off a big chunk.

"Because if it were, I'd have his balls fed to the birds."

Chloe wanted to laugh at that, but she knew better than even to crack a smile when her mother was this miffed.

"You're my only daughter, and I have to be present when you're being married off."

Chloe checked under the sink for leakages. There was none. She opened the pantry to steal a little part of the cake Mia had saved for William. She didn't hear Mia come up behind her. "Don't you dare, Chloe," she whisper-yelled.

"Please, Mia. Just a little," Chloe whispered back.

Mia obliged, cutting a piece of the cake for her then carrying the rest to the sitting room.

"Bitch," Mia muttered under her breath.

"I heard that," Chloe's voice came from the kitchen doorway.

"I meant for you to!" Mia and Karen's voices bellowed at the same time.

Chloe rolled her eyes and bit into the cake. Her mother would get tired soon and hang up. This wasn't the first time she got a lecture she wasn't interested in.

"Are you even listening to me, Chloe!" Karen said, sounding slightly exasperated.

"Yes, Mother," Chloe replied quickly, swallowing the last bit of the fluffy cake.

"So, tell me, whose idea was it?"

"It's mine, Mother. I just want a small wedding, and I've always wanted to get married in Jamaica," Chloe replied calmly. She needed her mom to see reason with her and not feel hurt by her decision to marry outside the State of New York.

"Always? But we've been together for the past 27 years, Chloe. When did it always start? After you met William?"

Chloe chuckled.

"You're lucky we're having this conversation over the phone, or else I would have spanked your ass," Karen said, sounding defeated.

Chloe couldn't tell her mother that her father knew about her wish to marry in Jamaica. He had supported her and promised to organize a surprise party for her and her husband once they returned to the State.

"I'm sorry, Mother," she said softly into the phone.

Karen was quiet for a long moment. She then released a long sigh. "It's okay, Baby. But promise me you'll come by the house before traveling?"

"Of course, Mom, I'll bring your god too," she said with a smile. She could hear her mother's smile too.

"You do that. I'll tell Stella and the girls."

Chloe chuckled. She could never wrap her head around how people in their seventies were called girls. But she couldn't tell her mother that. Karen would give her a lecture about women being girls forever, notwithstanding their age.

After a short pause, Karen asked, "Your girls going with you?"

"Yes, Mother."

" Good. I'm glad you have such powerful girls around you, Baby."

" I am too, for Stella and others," Chloe returned, her voice laced with emotions.

"Tell Mia she owes me to lunch on a yacht for not saying hi to me," she said and chuckled, " I know she came in the kitchen. I heard her. And I know that shit you do all the time when you think I'm giving you a lecture, Baby."

Chloe laughed. "Mom! Stop cussing!"

"You're all grown now and about to get hitched, so why not?"

They laughed together. Chloe wiped her eyes at the happy tears that were threatening to spill.

"Your father would have been so proud," Karen said, but her voice wasn't melancholic, and that pleased Chloe. She deserved to be happy and live for herself.

"He is, Mother. I see him every day."

They spoke about work, and the girls before Karen bade her daughter goodnight. "Tyler Perry' is waiting, Baby," she cooed cheerfully.

"Please, not you too," Chloe said, laughing. "Sleep well, mother."

"I love you."

"I love you too."

She stood in the kitchen for some minutes, staring at her phone, wishing she was at home with her mother, huddled on the couch and watching crappy TV series. Most times, Karen let her pick. She sighed, turned out the lights, and walked into the sitting room.

"That was entertaining," Mia snickered.

"Not funny, Babe," Chloe started, "I was kinda scared, you know?"

"That she wouldn't agree?"

Chloe nodded.

"I knew she would. Karen loves you more than anything in the world."

"Then why did she say so much?" Chloe asked her, brows furrowed in confusion.

"She's not pleased about missing your big day, but she's cool with whatever makes you happy," Mia said.

" Yeah, I guess."

She checked the door bolts and the back door and turned on the porch lights. "Have everything you need tonight?" she asked Mia, standing behind her on the couch.

"Yes," Mia replied, looking up at her "head in, Chloe. You have a man waiting for you."

"He's fast asleep," Chloe said.

"Then wake him up."

" How?" Chloe asked with faux ignorance.

"You're not that dumb, bitch. Go," Mia said, waving her off.

Chloe kissed her hair and ruffled it. "Call me if you need anything," Chloe said before retreating into her room, then closing the door behind her.

She got in beside William, snoring softly, and pulled the covers over them, wrapping her arms around his body. He was on his side, facing her.

She lay awake for some minutes, watching him sleep. She traced a hand down his neck, tickling him. She chuckled when he twisted his face, probably thinking a cockroach was crawling on his body. He made to turn and face the other side, but she held him tighter and kissed his forehead, her lips warm against his skin.

He snuggled in closer, his breath fanning her naked tits. She turned out the bedside lamp before sleep overtook her. That night, she didn't dream about Jamaica but her father. He was in the field in her backyard, helping her pick out the weeds. The flowers were fully bloomed, and the falling leaves covered the ground. Her father plucked a red rose and fixed it behind her right ear. His hands were soft against her skin that was dampened with sweat. He smiled into her eyes, the sight warming her heart. She smiled back and reached out to touch his wrinkled face, but he disappeared, leaving behind a feeling of warmth and the familiar scent of his cologne. She stirred awake, her body covered in sweat even though the room was cold.

CHAPTER FIVE

William sat down at the kitchen table with the cup of coffee Mia offered to him as soon as he stepped into the kitchen. Chloe was making a toast. She smiled over her shoulder at him, asked him if he slept well. Of course, he did. Spending the night in her arms, in her bed, was something he looked forward to every day. She was warm and soft. When he woke up that morning and found her beside him with her long blonde hair sprawled on the pillow, he had kissed her then, morning breath and all.

"I have to run home and do a few things before mid-day, guys," Mia said, picking up her handbag from the counter. She hugged Chloe and promised to meet up for lunch with the girls the following day. William rose and hugged her. "Have a nice day, Mia," he said, "and drive safe."

She gave him a salute." Yes, Sir." Then she trotted outside the kitchen, toward the front door.

William stalked over to Chloe and hugged her back. "Did you sleep okay?" he asked her.

"Yes, Will," she turned off the toaster, "what's your plan for today?"

"Nothing, I'll just stay here with you until 4 pm. I'm meeting up with my team for a meeting downtown."

"Okay." She poured coffee into a cup, then placed it in a tray and carried it to the kitchen table.

While they ate, William thumbed through the newspaper, stopping at intervals to sip his lemonade and munch on a toast. Sitting in silence, Chloe chewed slowly as she checked her phone and replied to work messages. Fatima had forwarded Mrs. Preston's reminder to her. She closed the tab and opened her call manager. The secretary picked up after the second ring and said he'd get back to her the following week.

"Everything okay?" William asked.

"Yes. Just work stuff."

"Okay." He dropped the newspaper on the chair beside him and picked up his cup, draining it in one gulp, and walked over to the sink to rinse it and set it to dry.

"Want to go to the beach?"

"Sure, the day is fucking sweltering."

William laughed easily. "It's summer, Babe."

"I know that, and I hate it," Chloe grumbled.

She loved the thick gray clouds, the sound of the wind, the droplets of rain on her window panes, the feeling of the cold tiles under her bare feet. Her chin lifted a fraction. "Want to see the small garden I started behind the house?" Chloe asked William, tilting her head sideways.

"I'd love to," he replied, then helped her up and draped his hands around her neck. "What did you plant?" he asked her, opening the back door that led to the backyard. An open space with a small field. He could spot the garden at the center of the field; the flowers were starting to bloom and looked watered.

"I water them every morning before breakfast," she intoned when she noticed his quizzical look.

"Wow, these are some beautiful flowers," he bent to take a closer look, "is that daylilies?" he asked, pointing at a plant with a yellow flower.

"Yes." She knelt beside him. "When I was younger, Dad and I used to have this little garden beside the house where we planted different kinds of flowers." She paused and pulled at a weed... "I was always confused between lilies and daylilies, so Dad had to take me to where we bought the two flowers' seedlings, and he taught me how to grow them." She missed her father and had been thinking about him a lot since the previous night at the party with David. She saw her father in him and realized she didn't think about him as often as she should.

William noticed her faraway look and pulled her into his arms. He sat down on the wet grasses with Chloe between his legs. The sun was out, but he didn't care. He wanted to stare at her while she looked at the flowers and thought about her father.

"We should go in," she said quietly after a long minute had passed.

He spotted a shade close to the fence with honeysuckles. The tree wasn't that tall, but just enough to keep the burning sun away. "Come on, let's go stay under that tree," he gestured toward the tree, pulling her up.

They walked slowly toward the tree. "You didn't tell me about this part of your house, Babe," William said.

"Yeah, I didn't venture out here until last month when I needed to get something from the backyard."

William sat down, leaned on the tree trunk, and then pulled her to sit between his legs. "Here, so I can smell your hair," he said, sniffing her hair.

She tipped her face upward and kissed his lips. "Want to talk about our trip now?" she asked.

He started playing with her fingers, "Of course." He tilted her head to the side to face him. "It's just going to be us, the girls, Craig, and the clergyman," he started.

"Yeah," she said.

Chloe told him about her wish to get tickets for the girls and book a room ahead.

"Of course, anything you want, Babe," he said, kissing her nose.

Her phone vibrated in her jean pocket, startling them apart.

"Ava," she said, thumbing the green button.

"Hello, Ava," she said, pushing away William when he tried to tickle her.

Ava wanted to be sure they were doing lunch the next day. Chloe said yes, then hung up. Ava was a tad distracted; Chloe could hear Andrea's voice in the background, demanding to be taken to the park. Chloe smiled, taking her hand to rest on her belly. She imagined a baby growing in there. With William, she was going to raise beautiful kids, ones they'd be proud of.

"We could get the tickets before lunch," William suggested.

Chloe seemed to mull it over before nodding. "That would be splendid," she gushed happily. "Thanks, Babe."

William brought out his phone and dialed a number. He murmured into the phone. "Yeah, thank you," he said before hanging up.

He turned to her. "Sam will bring them over this evening," he said, pulling her into his arms.

"Okay," she replied.

"Want to head in?" he asked, checking his Rolex.

"What time is it?"

"Noon," he said, standing up.

"Damn. Today is sure running faster than usual," she mused.

She held her hand out for him to help her up. "Still want to go to the beach?" he asked as they walked side by side down the grassy pathway that led to the house.

"No, when we get to Jamaica, we'll have enough of that," she blurted.

She poured them a glass of juice immediately as they got into the kitchen. William drank his in one gulp and stretched out his hand for more.

"Mia saved some cake for you last night," Chloe said, opening the fridge.

He bit into it, savoring the taste before chewing. "What did she put in this?" he queried, biting into it again.

" Salmon," Chloe said.

" Hmm, it's perfect."

Chloe nodded in response. She stepped into the hall when she heard the doorbell. Peeping through the window, she found her next-door neighbor. For all the years she'd been here in Georgia, she and this man had never exchanged more than two words. She wondered what he was doing knocking on her door.

"Hello, Mr. Francis," she greeted, blocking her doorway. He ignored her little tactics as his eyes were plastered on her boobs that were slightly exposed through the lacey tank top she wore.

"I, um," he stuttered. She noticed his gaze and pulled the loose shirt tightly around her. "I need to go out, and there's a car blocking mine."

Before she could reply, William's voice sounded behind her. "I'm sorry, man. I'll move it now." If he noticed the dick staring at her, he didn't comment on it. He kissed her fully on the lips. "Be right back, Babe," he said, winking at her.

Francis stalked ahead of him, his neck red with embarrassment. "You shouldn't do that, man," William said to him, his voice laced with anger.

"I'm sorry," Francis said, raising his palm in surrender.

William nodded. He realized he had forgotten the car key in his haste to go see who Chloe was talking with when he heard him mention a car blocking his. He cussed and told him to wait a moment.

Chloe was waiting behind him when he turned, her hands folded across her chest. "You were so green with envy that it clouded your eyes, huh?" she quipped, handing the key to him. He blushed shyly, causing her to laugh harder.

He opened the door and got into the driver's seat. "How about I just drive home from here?" he asked, lifting his brows.

"Go on, Babe, and come back for your phone later," she said, turning to go back into the house.

After William had moved the car, he went back into the house to find Chloe on the couch, shuffling through channels. He went to the minibar and poured himself a glass of scotch with ice. He drank slowly, watching her from the corner of his eyes as she cussed when she couldn't find her kind of movies.

He stifled a laugh, knowing she'd throw the remote at his head if he dared laugh at her pouty face.

He suggested they link her phone to the TV and watch a movie on Netflix instead.

Chloe settled for *The Ritual,* a movie that would scare the pants off most people but not Chloe.

She watched with keen interest the horrific escapades of the four friends. William brought her popcorn and sat beside her on the couch, nestling against her.

"Mia would have a nightmare for days if she watched this," Chloe said.

William chuckled. "Any normal person would," he returned. She smacked his head with the throw pillow.

"Y'all are just pussies," she said, glaring at him. William laughed and tried to stop the movie.

"Now I'm regretting making you watch this," he quipped.

Chloe kissed him. "Shut up and watch these men get killed."

"Eww, I'll have nightmares."

" Pussy," she mouthed, laughing at his facial expression.

CHAPTER SIX

William parked under the shade, then looked into his rear mirror to see anyone around. He was alone, just the way he liked it. He opened the door and stepped on the deserted road. There was a car parked 50 feet away from him, but there was no one else around the cemetery.

He picked up the basket full of flowers from the backseat and trotted down the grassy part to the stones marked with his dad, mom, and Rebecca. He knelt and removed the few weeds that were spurting from the stone.

"Hey, Dad," he said, dropping the yellow daylilies on his tomb. "Found this in Chloe's garden yesterday, and I figured you'd love them here."

The wind blew gently. It was chilly, even though the sun was glaring at him with such force. He rubbed his exposed arms, wishing he'd worn a coat instead.

He closed his eyes, envisioning his parents and Rebecca playing in a garden somewhere safe and free of the terror that existed in the world. He smiled when Rebecca looked over at him and blew him kisses, her blue eyes looking more radiant.

"I've agreed to get married in Jamaica," he said to Rebecca. She didn't say anything, just nodded and pointed at their mother.

William's voice caught in his throat when he saw the sad look in his mother's eyes. She was crying, the sobs wracking her body, making his dad put his arms around her. William saw his dad whisper something in his mother's ears. He couldn't hear them from where he stood but could see the smile on his mother's face. She turned to him, no longer in tears, but in its place was a smile so beautiful that he found himself smiling. In her eyes, he found acceptance.

"You should go home, boy; you've been kneeling in that position for the past 3 hours," a voice said, rousing him from whatever trance he was in.

A man who looked to be in his late sixties was brushing the tomb beside his father's. It looked like the man had already worked on his parents' and Rebecca's own, as they looked polished and devoid of weeds and dirt. The flowers he brought in a basket were arranged on the tombstone. The daylilies were on Rebecca's and not his father's, so he stood up and rearranged them. Putting the lilac on Rebekah's tomb, then the white rose for his mom and the daylilies for his father.

"My bad, I had no idea there were specifics," the man apologized, his voice low and calm like he was talking to a child.

William turned. "It's fine. Thanks for the help."

He picked himself up and walked down the pathway to his car. The other car was no longer there, and there was no other vehicle around. He turned to see the man still bent down in the same position he had left him. He wanted to ask him how he got here and who was picking him up, but he shook it off and opened his car door. That was when he noticed it, a truck parked at the other side. A little girl was sleeping in the passenger seat.

He sat in his car, replaying what he saw while at the cemetery. He didn't know what it was but was convinced that his parents never really left. He could still hear his mother's voice beckoning him to come downstairs for breakfast. He ignited the car and drove slowly down the deserted road—the chill from earlier seeping out from his body, replaced by the summer heat.

***

Ava was the first to arrive at the restaurant. She picked a table close to the windows and sat facing the doorway. She welcomed the iced tea the waitress offered and told her she was here for a meeting with her girls when the young woman asked her to place her order.

"Okay, Ma'am," she said and walked away.

Ava checked the group chat for new messages. One from Mia said she'd be late, as her house was on the outskirts of Georgia, 55 minutes away from the City.

'Rico looks hot asf in his this fitted shirts and blue jeans,' she typed and pressed send.

Mia was the first to reply.

'Damn, I'll be there in five!'

Avery dropped a series of laughing emojis and stickers.

'don't be a brat, Avery,' Olivia sent.

'Duh. You can't tell me what to do,' Avery replied to Olivia's bant.

Ava logged out of her messenger and placed the phone face down on the glass table. She was in no mood for those two.

She saw Chloe walk in, dressed in a red summer dress with dark sunglasses. Her hair was tied in a ponytail. The blond hair swung from side to side as she navigated the tables, heading toward Ava.

"Hey, Babe," Ava stood up to hug her, "you look exquisite in this red dress," she said, smiling broadly.

"Thank you. I love your perfume, new one?" Chloe asked, sniffing Ava's right wrist.

"Yes, Antonio got it for me on his last trip to Mexico," she gushed.

Ava pulled out the chair next to her. "Come sit and tell me about this man of yours. It's been ages since I last saw him."

Chloe laughed and placed her bag behind her. "I update all of you on messenger all the time; stop acting like you don't see those messages. You just want to see me blush," Chloe said, rolling her eyes.

"I love it when you blush, Chloe. It brings out the rosy color in your cheeks, making you look like a flower watered with pearls," Ava gushed, her deep brown eyes assessing Chloe. "You look delighted," she added, noticing the glow on Chloe's face.

"And that's without the sex; imagine when they start shagging. She's going to be plastered on Vogue with the headline, 'Glow Queen,'" Mia intoned, sitting down on the vacant chair beside

Chloe. She looked around the room, searching for Rico. "Where is he, Ava?" she asked, her eyes still roaming.

"I'm fine, Mia. Did you fly down here?" Ava quizzed, taking a sip of her tea.

"No, I drove. I have a car, remember?" Mia returned, waving at the waitress idling over at the counter.

"Oh shit. I forgot that bit," Ava countered, "but your message said..."

"I know what I sent, thank you very much," Mia cut in.

Chloe watched them with keen interest, her arms folded on the table.

"Enjoying the show, bride-to-be?" Ava managed between a laugh that was bubbling from her inside.

"Please, carry on," Chloe returned, her lips quirking in a smile.

"The spicy margarita," Chloe told the waitress who had walked over to their side while they chatted. As was the name on the tag pinned to her white shirt, Stacie turned to Mia.

"Ma'am?"

"What drink do you recommend, Stacie?" Mia asked, placing her forefinger under her chin.

"Um, the blueberry bramble," Stacie said suggestively.

Mia nodded. " I'll take it. Make it two."

Stacie nodded and went off to the bar.

"Two?" Chloe asked.

Mia rolled her eyes. "I'm not a drunk, Chloe. Look behind you."

They all did. Olivia was heading toward them. Her phone to her left ear as she walked toward them, waving at a couple eating at the other side of the room. She muttered a bye as she got closer to them. "Hello, girls." She hugged Chloe first, then Ava and Mia last. I'm sorry I was caught up in traffic."

"Of course, dick traffic," Mia muttered under her breath. Chloe, who sat closer to her, heard and laughed, smacking Mia's knee under the table.

"Where's Avery?" Olivia asked, sitting down beside Ava.

"She's on her way," Ava said, then drained her cup in one last gulp. "God, I could use a dip in the beach right now," she said.

"But you just had an iced tea," Chloe said.

"I'm thinking about the life after now. The iced tea is going to finish," Ava returned

The girls laughed.

"We should order," Mia said, picking up the menu

"No, let's wait for Avery," Olivia said.

The waitress came then with their drinks. Mia offered the second glass to Olivia.

"Thanks," she said, taking a sip. "Blueberry bramble," she moaned. "It's my new favorite," she added when she noticed the girls staring at her.

Avery arrived then, dressed in shorts and a shirt twice her size.

"Hey girls," she greeted, going around for hugs and kisses.

"You okay?" Mia asked, touching her arm.

"Yes. The traffic was crazy. Had to make a detour," she said and sat down on the only vacant chair that was between Olivia and Mia.

She exhaled slowly. "What's that, Chloe?" she asked, pointing at Chloe's drink.

"Spicy margarita," Chloe replied.

"Sounds fancy, I'll take it," Avery said, then beckoned to the waitress that was hovering around the table.

"I'll have the spicy heaven my friend is having." Stacie nodded and asked the others if they were ready to order.

"Food first?" Avery asked, looking around at the others.

"No, the news first. I've been craving it since Mia told me about Jamaica," Ava said, smiling mischievously

" Mia!!" Chloe bellowed, turning to glare at her.

Mia shrugged unapologetically. "She offered to let me borrow her cowboy boots." At the girls' disgruntled look, she continued. "The one with glitters all over."

"Oh," Olivia quipped, "I'd have done the same thing. Those boots are spectacular."

Mia snickered. "You see, it's a gem." She picked up her glass and took a large sip. "Food first, I'm starving."

"Me too," Avery chirped in.

Chloe lifted a finger, beckoning their server.

"Ready to order now?" Stacie asked, patting her black skirt nervously.

"Yes, Stacie," Ava said, then pointed at number three on the menu, "I'll have that."

Stacie looked over at Chloe.

"Um, BLT," Chloe said without looking at the menu.

"You should try something else, Chloe. Ain't you tired of eating those?" Olivia quipped.

Chloe rolled her eyes, waving her off. "I will after you've ordered something different apart from a Reuben sandwich, alright?"

Ava asked for an Apple pie, and Avery settled for baked Alaska.

When Stacie looked at Olivia, Mia laughed. "You heard what Chloe said, Stacie; bring the girl a Reuben sandwich." The girls laughed, Olivia glaring intensely at Mia.

"What's yours, Ma'am?" Stacie asked Mia.

"Um, I think you should ask your boss; he knows what I like," Mia said, twirling the straw in her drink.

"Mia, just tell the girl," Ava intoned.

"Or she could call him for me instead?" Mia said, looking at Stacie, "could you do that?"

"Um, Ma'am... I"..." Stacie stuttered, not knowing how to tell Mia that Rico's girlfriend was around, and they were together in his office.

"Stacie," Olivia called. Stacie looked over at her. "It's Philly cheesecake. Go on now."

Stacie stalked away as fast as her legs could carry her.

"That was crazy, girls," Avery said, laughing silently.

"Mia!" Chloe bellowed, making the girls jump.

"Duh, Chloe. You brought us here. You could have picked the diner or Mason's café," Mia countered.

" I'm sorry, next time, we'll lunch in Italy," Chloe said, her eyes narrowing.

"Far from Rico's charm," Olivia chirped in with a small laugh.

"Hello, ladies," Rico's voice sounded behind Chloe. The girls didn't notice him as they were engrossed in banter. Mia sat up straight and rearranged her hair, patting the sides gently. She smiled up at Rico, who returned it and asked if they had been attended to.

"Yes, Stacie is an angel," Olivia said, then sipped her drink that was no longer cold. She drained the cup and pushed it aside to keep her hand on the table.

"Yeah, she new?" Chloe queried.

"Yes. She's my cousin," Rico returned. He looked happy that they were complimenting his cousin. She just came in from Africa, where she did her masters and ways of working for a few months before setting up her own business.

"Wow, no wonder she's so pretty and well mannered," Mia cooed, "it must run in the family," she looked up at Rico and winked. "Right?" she asked, drumming her finger on the glass. Her fingers were painted red, and the tips were long and penciled. She wanted Rico to notice it, and he did. He smiled, his eyes warming slightly. "Yes, Mia," he said, removing his eyes from hers.

" So, if you girls need anything......" he started.

" We'll call you...got it," Ava said, laughing.

" You know the drill. " He smiled at Ava. "You ladies enjoy your meal," he said, turning to walk away.

"Thanks, Rico," the girls said in unison.

They were silent for a few minutes, each engrossed in her drink. Olivia, who had finished hers, brought out her phone to check her Instagram.

"Wow, I need another of this drink," Ava said after draining her glass. She relaxed her back onto the leather chair and patted her belly. "It's the best thing I've tasted in years," she added

Chloe chuckled. "... the same thing you said about sex on the beach."

"And The Winston cocktail," Mia said slowly, glancing up from her empty glass.

"This one is my new favorite," Ave countered with a wry grin. "Y'all should stop being so pissy."

Stacie cleared her throat behind Chloe, whose back was to the counter. "Here," she placed their food in front of them," want anything to drink. Wine? Water? Juice?"

"Tell Rico to choose for us," Avery said, opening her food, "wow, this looks amazing."

"You eat that all the time, Ava, get used to it," Olivia said, opening hers. She inhaled and exhaled loudly. "I Love Rico's," she purred.

With an amused nod, Stacie walked back to the counter.

The girls were in silence, chewing slowly.

"I need a drink," Avery said, glancing up at the counter.

"She's coming. Sorry," Chloe said before taking a huge bite of her bacon."

With a tray filled with drinks balanced expertly on her arms, Stacie stopped at their table.

She placed the tray down with ginger passion, Julia's blush, Mai tai, and watermelon cooler.

"Thank you, Stacie," Avery said, patting her hand gently, "and welcome to Georgia."

"Thank you," Stacie said, beaming. She was beautiful and had the body of a dancer. Olivia envied her long-toned legs and curvature.

"You are gorgeous!" Olivia blurted before she could stop herself. The girls smiled and nodded in affirmation.

Stacie blushed shyly. Being complimented by many beautiful, successful young women wasn't something she was used to. Most ladies she had met envied her body and tried to avoid her, so she wouldn't 'snatch their men.' If only they knew she was a lesbian and would rather drown in a pond than let a man put his hands on her. She had asked Rico earlier about the blond. She had learned her name was Chloe, and she was getting married soon to a William Stanford. Stacie looked around the table at the women. They were all so beautiful and elegantly dressed. Simple too. Her eyes met the redhead, and she winked. Mia, Rico said she was feisty. *She's probably a firecracker in bed,* Stacie mused, her palm getting sweaty. She smiled at Mia and fought hard not to wink back. The woman was perhaps joking around and didn't know the consequences of her little action.

"Thank you," she said and bowed slightly before leaving them to their meals. She could hear Mia asking the rest if they'd seen Rico. Stacie chuckled. If only she knew. Rico was in his office getting a blow job from Aurora, his black American girlfriend. They'd be out soon, and Stacie couldn't wait to see the look on Mia's face. Rico would lose a customer and a crush he was probably oblivious to, and it was a pity. Stacie wished she were in his shoes.. she'd jump on Mia. The woman was gorgeous and had the perfect body.

Chloe pushed her plate away and leaned her back against the chair. She looked around the table, Avery was almost done, and Olivia cleared up her plate. Mia was on her phone, her lips between her teeth. She was probably reading one of those erotic stories she was so crazy about.

Chloe took a deep breath and released slowly.

"It's time," Ava said, pushing her plate away. "We need wine, something strong," she added, sipping her drink.

"Yeah, we should. Only God knows what Chloe is going to dump on us," Olivia said nonchalantly.

"It's Jamaica, Liv. Mia's mentioned it already," Avery said, patting Olivia's knees under the table.

Chloe ignored Olivia and went ahead to give out the envelopes she had brought to the girls.

"Those are your tickets," she said, smiling broadly, "the rooms have been booked, and a tour guide is on standby to show us around," she added gleefully.

"Damn!" Ava muttered, opening the pamphlet that was attached to the tickets.

"You'll find all the exotic places in there," Chloe said, pointing at the pamphlet. "When we get there, we'll tour the whole place," she added, looking at their faces to gauge their reactions. What she saw delighted her immensely. The girls were pleased and looked eager. She jumped in her seat and clapped her hands excitedly.

"I'd rather spend my entire day at one of these beaches than go touring," Ava said, looking through the pictures of Negril Beach and others. "God, can y'all see this," she said, pointing at the clear water and white Sand, "when are we leaving, Chloe?" she asked, facing Chloe with her eyes wide.

"I thought you said....." Ava started, her eyes twinkling with mischief.

"I know what I said, Ava, save it. I'm just so excited right now," Olivia retorted.

"We all are," Avery said, smiling, "I mean girrrlllll, this place is sick!"

"I'm glad y'all like it," Chloe said. She beckoned to the waitress. "A bottle of a legacy by Angostura."

"We are going high," Mia sang, ignoring Olivia's stare down.

"Just a glass for you, Mia. You're taking me home. I didn't come in my car," Ava said.

"You'll take another cab. I'll pay," Mia returned.

Chloe hushed them. "What color should I use for my wedding dress?"

"Pink," Mia suggested abruptly.

"Oh please, she'd look like a dollhouse," Avery said.

"Blue," Olivia suggested.

"Yeah, it will match William's eyes," Avery added.

Stacie brought the wine in an ice bucket with glasses.

"You're an expert at this, Stacie," Mia intoned, "done this before?" she asked, accepting the glass Stacie offered to her.

Stacie blushed. "Yes, when I was in college," she said.

After Stacie had made sure that everyone had a glass in their hands, she returned to the counter with the tray.

"So," Chloe drawled, "is blue okay?" she asked, looking around at everyone.

They all nodded. "And I have the perfect dress picked just for you," Olivia said, unlocking her phone. She pulled up a picture of a blue dress in a hanger. It was a blur chiffon gown, open at the back and sleeveless.

"This would look spectacular on you, girl," Avery cooed.

"Thank you, Olivia," Chloe said, her eyes Misty. "I've been trying to come up with the perfect sketch, and nothing was forthcoming," she dabbed at her eyes, "thanks, Liv."

Olivia nodded and patted her hands across the table. "Anything for you. All of you, girls," she said, turning her eyes at all of them.

"Thank you," Mia mouthed. She nodded.

Avery raised her wine glass. "Now, let's toast." She looked around to make sure everyone was holding theirs.

"To Jamaica," she said.

"To Jamaica," the girls chorused.

They drank it in one gulp then poured another round.

"Totally worth the money," Chloe said, licking her lips.

Stacie came over to clear the plates and drop the bill. Chloe rummaged in her purse, then handed some money worth more than the food and asked her to keep the change. "You're so cool, Stacie," Chloe insisted when Stacie refused the 20$ tip. "Keep it. Please." Stacie nodded and thanked her again.

Just then, Mia spotted Rico with a woman. She had his arms around him, possessively. Not the kind she was used to seeing. Mia perked up, and her eyes narrowed in annoyance and jealousy. She found Stacie leaning against the door that led to the back, staring at Rico and the girl, then at her. Bitch was expecting drama. She probably assumed something was going on between Mia and her cousin because Mia said earlier. Mia looked away, picking up her wine glass. The girls were unaware of what was transpiring as Ava was pointing out the number of parishes in Jamaica and trying to decide which to use for Chloe's wedding. "Not a lot, compared to New York City," Avery was saying, pointing at a picture on her phone screen.

Chloe nudged Mia. "You okay?" The others looked up from Avery's phone and toward Mia.

"Yeah," Mia said without blinking.

"Hm-hm," Olivia paused as if she was trying to make up her mind about speaking, "you've been staring at that spot for the past 5 minutes,"

"I'm just thinking. You know, processing my thoughts," Mia said like she was explaining the alphabet to a child. Olivia rolled her eyes and told her to go to hell.

"Easy girls, whatever it is, she'll tell us later," Avery said, trying to appease the situation. It wasn't unusual, as the girls fought all the time and made up immediately after, but that wasn't the time they tried to decide when would be appropriate for them to board the plane.

"I can now if y'all would just look behind you," Mia said, her eyes narrowing.

They all turned back. "Damn, that's not what I expected," Chloe whispered conspiratorially like she was sharing a big secret.

"Huh, what were you expecting?" Mia asked, turning to face Chloe.

"She's pretty hot," Olivia said, then sipped her wine, her eyes avoiding Mia's.

"Yeah, right," Mia said. Chloe could read something in her voice, but it wasn't hurt. She was sad, yes, but that was just about it. There was no disappointment, no hard feelings. Chloe thought it was just a mild crush, sipping her wine and looking over the rim at Mia, who was engrossed in her half-finished glass of wine.

"You okay, Babe?" she asked, love, coloring her words.

" Yes, it's nothing really," Mia said softly.

" So," Chloe started breaking the silence, "we'll leave the day after tomorrow." She paused as if waiting for one of them to object. They kept mute, urging her silently to continue. "You can use tomorrow to pack, do last-minute shopping, and wrap up your work stuff. Is that okay?"

"Of course," Mia chirped. Her dark mood was forgotten and replaced with the Mia they were used to. Chloe smiled at her and winked.

"That's okay," Avery seconded, smiling pleasantly. The others nodded. Chloe could tell they were all excited about the trip and her mood soared. These girls, this group, she could do anything for them.

"Congratulations, Chloe." A deep, laughter-filled voice sounded behind them. It was Rico, in the company of his lady friend. He introduced her to them, and the girls smiled and welcomed her. She was a black American with the body of a model. Mia even complimented her long black hair. "Love yours too. Red hairs are so beautiful to look at," Aurora said to Mia, reaching out to touch a tendril of her red hair that was loosely around her shoulders.

"Congratulations, Chloe," Aurora said, turning to Chloe with a smile and a twinkle in her eyes.

"Thank you, Aurora." Chloe smiled warmly.

Rico excused himself and left with his girlfriend. To Chloe, he promised to keep in touch and await her return after the ceremony in Jamaica. "I'll miss you, ladies," he said quietly.

Chloe smiled, considering her next words carefully. "We'll be back before you know it, Rico," she said, patting his hand gently.

The duo walked away. The restaurant was filled up, and a group of guys was beside them arguing about politics. Chloe turned to the girls; they were on the last glass of wine. Ava and Olivia went through the pamphlet, gushing at the beaches and exotic sights.

Her phone vibrated on the table; it was William. Probably called to know if the girls were okay with going to Jamaica. If only he knew. They'd go anywhere with a beach and bars.

"Hello, Babe," she said softly into the phone

" Hey, gem. You okay?" he asked, his baritone ringing into her ears like a soft melody.

"Yes." She paused and looked around at the girls. They were talking about what they'd do, Olivia was excited about the John Crow Batty. A famous Jamaica rum known for its strong taste and alcohol level. Chloe made a mental note to keep them away from it as it was said to be way too strong in the articles she'd read online. "Are you are at work?" she asked William, removing her gaze from the girls to focus on her manicured fingernails that were painted blue and nude.

"Yes, but I'll be heading home soon," William said. He sounded tired.

"Want me to come over?" she asked, even when she knew the answer already.

"Yes, please," he said, his need for her dripping off his words. She smiled, ignoring the girl's look of faux astonishment.

"I'll be there when you get home." She could hear him exhaling roughly and picture his shoulders relaxing.

"I love you, gem," he whispered into the phone.

Her lips tilted in an impish smile. "I love you too," she breathed, then hung up.

"Giirrrllll, I felt that shit you just did there!" Ava exclaimed.

Chloe reddened.

"The day you all are going to fuck, the world will explode from the intensity of it. Damn!" Mia added quickly, reverting her eyes from Chloe's direction.

Chloe shot them a lopsided grin. "You girls are so silly. Talking about my sex life like I'm not here." She stood up and put her purse under her armpit. "I'll have to be home before he gets back," she said, pushing her chair backward and moving away from the take.

They all stood up; Olivia drained her glass and Ava's. "I can't wait to drink more of that in Jamaica." Enthusiasm colored her words. "It's going to..."

"We'll have John Crow Batty instead," Mia cut in, a slow smile spreading across her face.

"Whatever," Olivia said, waving away Mia's interruption.

The girls walked out of the restaurant, Chloe behind, typing rapidly on her phone. If there was a way she could keep the damn John Crow Batty from the girls, she'd do it in a heartbeat. Mia was looking forward to the drink more than the beaches. She sighed, rubbing her forehead as if to pacify the turmoil she was going through at the thought of them getting shamelessly drunk or poisoned. Babysitting wasn't in the cards. *God help me*, she mused.

CHAPTER SEVEN

William was stretched out on the couch, watching a commentary on the television. Happy to be on leave from work, at least for the next two months. David had surprised him when he suggested William rake the rest of the week off even though he was due to travel the following week. The old man voiced his displeasure at having to miss his wedding to 'such a beautiful and intelligent woman' as were his words.

He smiled, his lips twisting at the sides as he thought about how refreshing it was when he first touched her, the warmth that spread throughout his body when she muttered his name at the airport. Unlike the women before her, after Pamela, he was always skeptical and kept them at arm's length, not wanting to make a mistake twice. The first one gave him his boy, and he wanted to do things right this time.

The emptiness had lessened, in its place, was this overwhelming feeling of fulfillment and companionship. Chloe made him want to do better and love life more. He shifted onto his side to watch the commentary as it was almost wrapping up. He needed to go shopping - early Christmas presents to Craig's parents. He was leaving the day after Thanksgiving, which was November 24th, to join Chloe and the girls leaving a week before him and Craig. They agreed to spend their Christmas in Jamaica and get to see a few places before he arrived. His mind and gaze drifted from the television to a spot at the corner of the room, where the sunlight was filtering in from the opened windows.

William's phone beeped with a message; he picked it up quickly, hoping it to be an update from Chloe about their flight since they were e route to Jamaica. It wasn't, but it was something good too. A picture of his son in what looked like a mini car, he was the driver, and his mom was waving at him from the sideline. He smiled and sent a quick thank you to Rosie, Craig's mother. She had taken Pamela and Stanford to Chicago; they were to spend their Thanksgiving there and return to the States two days after Thanksgiving. Rosie wanted to get Pamela out of the way so that she wouldn't make trouble for him at the airport.

He heaved a heavy sigh as his forefinger massaged his forehead. Thinking about Pamela incited a migraine every damn time.

"Yo, Champ!" Craig bellowed, coming into the sitting room. "Want to grab a few things at the store? Do you want to come with?" he asked William.

" No, you go ahead. I'll go to the mall later to grab a few gifts," William said wryly.

You good?"

William nodded. "Just thinking about stuff."

"Don't stress it, bro. We're getting you married soon," Craig said.

" Yeah. See you later," William returned.

After Craig had left, he checked his phone again for messages from Chloe. There was one, short but enough to calm his nerves.

'Just arrived at the Montego Bay's Donald Sangster International Airport. We'll call once we settle in.'

He released a breath he didn't know he was holding, typed a quick reply, and then pressed send. He needed to make a few plans for the days he'd be staying at home before going over to Anderson's and traveling.

William stood up from the couch and walked into his kitchen to prepare a meatball sandwich. It's been a while he had one. He brought out the veggies and was about rummaging for the other ingredients when his housekeeper walked in.

"Let me handle that, William," Felix said, taking the veggies from him and turning on the tap.

William couldn't argue, so he left and walked back to the couch to resume watching the television. This time, he settled for a movie that starred his favorite actor, Ryan Rodney Reynolds. He called Felix to get him a scotch. "Neat, with ice," he added, picking up the remote to increase the volume.

Craig came back before he got to the middle of the movie, and with him was a blonde with fake tits. She was scantily dressed in a cropped top and shorts that barely covered her bum. He gave Craig an annoyed look when her back was turned to him.

Craig shrugged, his face expressionless.

"Can I have one of that?" she asked, pointing at William's drink. Craig nodded and stalked off to get her a drink from the minibar.

"You a doctor?" she asked pointedly.

He stalled like he was weighing his answer, then took a look sip. "No....."

"Josefina," she said, interrupting him with a smile that looked almost painful. William cringed, wondering where Craig picked her up from.

"You've not answered my question'?" she crooned, batting her lashes. He wanted to laugh out loud at her poor attempt at flirting with him. Craig wasn't even into threesomes, so what the hell was this girl babbling about?

Craig took longer than normal to mix a damn drink. He was whistling under his breath.

William hesitated then said, "No, I'm a soldier."

She was about to say something when Craig came back with her drink. William exhaled and grabbed his half-finished drink, draining it in one gulp, then excused himself to rinse the glass.

"He's charming," Josefina said with a wry grin. "I'd assumed he was a doctor with all the neat nails and trimmed hair," she added conspiratorially. Craig chuckled humorlessly. "Stay away from him, Josefina; he's getting married next month." Craig's tone sounded slightly annoyed and irritated. He had noticed the flirtatious looks she threw William's way when he was over at the bar making her a drink.

She leaned forward and smiled; her dazzling smile looked nothing like the sun streaming from the window. It was filled with contempt, hate, and what Craig couldn't place. He had seen her at the store, and she was all over him like a pest. Offering to blow him and make him cum more times than he could count. What single man turned down a good time with a woman that looked that bad-ass, so he had agreed, and there she was, on Williams's case, acting all flirty and deadly.

She crawled over to him on her knees and got between his legs. "I think it's time for that blow job I promised you, or would you rather invite your friend to play with us?" she asked, the corner of her mouth quirking in a sardonic smile. He wanted to spit in her face and ask her to leave, but instead, he pulled her by the hair. "Kinky, like that," she cooed.

He drew her face closer to his. "Now, you'll stand up and get the fuck out of here before I throw you out," he thundered. His face was red with anger and disgust.

She scrambled away, looking at him with her seductive eyes that had turned to that of a character in a horror movie. "You'll hear from me soon, Craig," she said over her shoulder, grinning cockily. The door opened and closed with a bang. Craig sighed and carried her untouched drink, gulping it down at once.

"You'll need more than that next time you invite a whore into this house, Craig," William barked, with disbelief in his eyes.

Craig stared at him for a long while, then nodded, be knew arguing at that point with William was not something he should do. "I'm sorry, Champ. I had no idea she was gon' be trouble," he said gently.

The unexpected turn of events caught him by surprise. He had expected Craig to lecture him about letting loose and living. He shrugged. "Next time, ask them if they're mentally stable. That one was a nutcase," his tone rang firm.

Craig nodded and apologized again.

"Do you want to eat out here or in the kitchen?" Felix asked from the kitchen doorway.

" In the kitchen, Felix," William said, glancing briefly at Craig, "it's meatball sandwich, if you would like to have one or would you rather have a psycho blow you?" he added in a teasing tone.

Craig rolled his eyes and glared at William. "That's not even funny," he returned, fighting the faint beginning of a smile. William laughed, his baritone voice vibrating throughout the house.

"You should have seen her face when I refused to acknowledge her," William said, his eyes sparkling with humor.

Craig cast him a quelling glance then pulled out a kitchen stool. "This looks delicious, Felix," he said, biting off a corner of the sandwich.

"You should thank me, it was my idea," William said smugly.

"Go to hell," Craig muttered under his breath before taking a big chunk of the sandwich.

CHAPTER EIGHT

Chloe leaned against the bed headboard in her suite at the Azul Beach Resort in Negril. William had picked one just a few minutes walk to the beaches. She savored a sense of anticipation - the girls were here in Jamaica with her, and she was getting married in a few weeks to the man of her dreams.

She remembered her visit to her mother. Karen had invited her 'girls,' and they were all there to fawn over William. She ruse from the bed and paced the room, checking out the bathroom, ensuite sitting room, and the sockets. She brought out her laptop and plugged it in to charge. William had said no working, but she needed to keep tabs and meet her clients' needs, or at least try to.

Chloe walked to the double window and looked into the Streets. She was jet-lagged and needed to sleep, but she was curious. Her mind kept replaying the dream she had before making the trip down here. She peered into the brightly lit streets with people walking on the sidewalk and the cars driving carefully down the streets, not fast-paced like New Yorkers.

"Wow!" She let out a gasp when she saw the Negril beach. It was spectacular, and the colorful lights around the beach gave it this beautiful glow, enchanting even. She took a picture and sent it to William.

'Damn, that looks absolutely perfect. Not as much as you do, gem,' he replied.

She laughed and shook her head slowly, muttering an inaudible word. She was just about type in a reply when her phone beeped the second time. It was William:

'I can't wait to fuck you there. The thought of me. inside of you under these lights is making me really hard."

She could feel the heat between her legs, spreading upward.

'I'm sure looking forward to being possessed by you. The thought of your body on mine is making my insides explode with need.' She pressed send. Leaning her tummy carefully on the window pane.

'You shouldn't be doing that, gem. I'll see you in a few days.' She reread the text, a wry grin playing on her red-painted lips. She was about to reply when the door was swung open; she twirled away to find the girls dressed in shorts and looking all ready to go out. "We didn't make any plans," Chloe said, staring at them simultaneously, "or did I miss something," she added, pushing away from the window. Mia took her spot, leaning slightly to peer into the ground below.

"You should be careful," Avery chided her gently.

"You should see this," Mia retorted, "damn, this place is spectacular," she added.

Ava came over to stand beside her, "come on, Mia. Chloe says we can't go out tonight. She's jet-lagged."

"She is? Or she wants to stay in and make love to her boo?" Olivia said, lifting an eyebrow at Chloe.

Chloe giggled and waved her comment off. "Just really need to sleep, girls," she said, slumping on the well-made bed with white linens and a red duvet that was big enough for ten persons. The mahogany wood was polished and had Jamaica drawing inscribed on it. She ran her hand on a Bob Marley's wood portrait on the headboard.

"Heard his brother is playing soon at um," Avery said as she noticed the drawing, then opened her phone and pulled up a flyer, "Negril Beach... I .."

"That's the beach over there," Chloe cut in, pointing at the beach she was staring at before they came in.

The girls squealed delightfully

"I can't wait. I love his music," Mia said with so much enthusiasm. Avery made a gagging sound, "You don't, Mia. You just want to go mingle with men."

Mia opened her mouth then closed it again, looking like a child caught with a dildo, then she squared her shoulders and shrugged nonchalantly. "It makes no difference to me, Avery," she finally ground out, waving her polished red nails flippantly.

Chloe slipped through the door onto the balcony to escape the argument set to erupt. The night air was therapeutic as it blew across her face and hair. She closed her eyes and breathed in the scent of the beach - it was briny and had a calmy effect on her.

Chloe's phone vibrated with a message. "William," she sighed his name before typing a reply:

'They're Inside; I'm on the balcony, thinking about you,' she sent.

'Video call?' his response was quick and eager.

'Okay,' she texted back, then adjusted the strapless top she had on to show the top of her cleavage, then searched around for the light switch. Finding one on the wall close to her, she turned it on before pressing the accept button on the phone screen.

"Hello, Darling," she breathed sexily, playing with a tendril of her long blonde hair that was falling around her face due to the night breeze.

He was silent for a long minute, and when he spoke, she relaxed against the railing, her back to the beach. At that moment, all she wanted to focus on was his voice - the sound of his laugh. The way his lips moved. She blanked out on the chatter around her and nodded silently to the question he was asking, staring intensely into his brown eyes that were screaming with love just for her.

CHAPTER NINE

"Hello, what can I get for you ladies?" a woman with a plus-size body on a blue apron over her pink gown asked in a thick Jamaican accent. She was heavily made up and had on the longest lashes Chloe had ever seen.

"Um, what do you recommend for lunch.. we're new here?" Chloe replied, smiling broadly, the way her mama taught her.

"Oh, the New Yorkers," she drawled, her smile widening. "I'm Sheng, the manager of this bar."

Chloe wondered what a manager was doing serving the patrons. She laughed when she noticed the puzzled look on Chloe's face

"My girls saw you ladies and came to call me," she placed her right hand on the table, "you see, we have this policy about the manager attending to the visitors on their first day, that way, we'd get to interact and tell you about the hotel plans for the holiday season."

"Wow...that's brilliant," Avery said, pausing her TikTok video to take a closer look at the woman.

"Thank you," Sheng beamed at them. "So, what would you like?" she asked, her eyes twinkling as she deftly pushed the menu toward Chloe. "They're written in English," she added quickly.

"I know that, but we," Chloe started, waving her hands at the girls, "want you to recommend, Sheng." The girls let out a laugh at her pronunciation.

"I have an English name," Sheng said, stifling a laugh, "Selina."

"Celina," Chloe said, "we'll take whatever you recommend."

Sheng nodded. "Okay."

She walked briskly away, her 5-inch heels making small sounds on the wooden floor.

"Oh. My. God," Ava whispered, "I've never seen someone so big and looking that good."

"Hm-hm," Mia muttered," she's so beautiful, and her accent is thick asf."

Chloe rolled her eyes. "Someone should open the pamphlet, please. We are going exploring today," she said, pushing the pamphlet toward the center of the glass table.

Olivia picked it up and skimmed through the pages before stopping at a picture. "Um, we should go visit the haunted house."

"Rose Hall Great House?" Sheng asked, coming back to their table with a bottle of wine in an ice bucket and a waitress behind her holding a tray with wine glasses.

"Yes." Olivia nodded.

"   You should see it at night; the owner who passed away was called the White Witch of Rose Hall," Sheng added in a low, conspiratorial tone.

"Wow," Chloe watched the waitress open the wine and pour it into the glasses. When she got to her, Chloe touched her hand briefly. "What's this called?" she asked in a monotone so as not to disrupt the other's ongoing conversation, but Sheng heard her and turned to her with her signature manager smile. The kind that is forced but doesn't look forced.

"It's sparkling, Shiraz."

Chloe nodded and thanked her. "Just a little," she told her waitress.

"So, we can't go there during the day?" Mia asked, looking expectantly at Sheng.

Sheng smiled and nodded. "You can; it's just not going to be that scary, you know?"

The girls nodded and agreed to go after lunch.

"Speaking of lunch," Sheng said excitedly, "There are varieties you ladies will have to pick."

Chloe was a tad pissed at the *'You ladies…you ladies.'* She wished Sheng would calm down and ask for their names since they were obviously going to stay there for a few weeks.

"Um." Chloe started clearing her throat to draw Sheng's attention. When Sheng focused her eyes on her, Chloe smiled. "Thank you." She beamed with a slight polite nod; the other woman smiled back and urged her with her eyes to say whatever was on her mind.

"I'm Chloe, and that is Mia." She pointed out the girls and mentioned their names. "I figured we'll be here for a while, so it'd be best if you knew our names, Selina," Chloe said. "Just in case," she added quickly with a wide grin.

Sheng nodded and thanked her. "You have lovely names. Maybe I should change mine to Avery?" she asked smartly in her thick accent. She made the name sound like poetry.

Avery laughed lightly and nodded her head. "Selina is cool, Sheng. Stick to it."

Sheng smiled at her then snapped her fingers. A waiter appeared, pushing a trolley of food.

"Chloe, I'm sorry. I couldn't decide on anything," she told the young man to place the foods on the table, "these are all good and will go well with the rum."

Ava opened her mouth in wonder. "All these for just lunch?" she asked, opening the first plate that was wrapped with a foiled paper. "Wow… this looks alive," she said, pointing at the crabs.

Sheng threw back her head and laughed. "That's ackee and codfish," she explained slowly. "And we also have jerk chicken, pork, fish, pepper pot soup, rice and peas, jerk shark, and oxtail."

The girls were in awe as they stared at the truckload of food. In New York, one would just grab a sandwich and be done with lunch, but it looked like Jamaicans went all out.

"What's for dessert?" Mia asked, supporting her head with her balled fist.

"Bulla cake," Sheng said, clapping excitedly.

"Enjoy your meal, ladies. And please, press that button if you need anything," Sheng said.

"Thank yuh," Chloe said with the tiniest bit of Jamaican accent she could muster.

Sheng smiled and nodded politely before walking back to the front of the room.

Chloe looked around for the first time. The room was beautifully decorated with Jamaican colors. She spotted a massive painting of a sea and people surrounded by incredible creatures lying on the white sand.

She noticed that they were secluded from other patrons and the glass partition was soundproof as she could see the couple laughing loudly but heard no sound. That means the girls can be as loud as they want without attracting unnecessary attention. Mia nudged her gently. "You okay, Chloe?"

She nodded with a big smile that brought out her dimple. "I am, Mia. And thankful too." She really was glad that William picked the best place for them to stay. The suites were top-notch, with exquisite views from the balcony and the windows.

"So, where are we going first?" Ava asked, taking a huge bite of the jerk chicken. "Hmm, it's delicious," she moaned, glancing at the others as they were a tad skeptical about eating the foreign meals to avoid food poisoning.

"Let's go to the haunted house," Avery suggested. "We're here for Chloe, and she's into those horror shit," she added with a dramatic eye roll.

"Y'all can do whatever. I'm just here to get married to the best man alive," Chloe returned.

She settled for the rice and peas, dishing two spoons full into her plate.

"Oh yeah," Olivia said, reaching across from her to pick up the chicken and add to her pepper pot soup.

"What's the other option?" Ava asked.

"There's Frenchman cove, Blue Lagoon, Reach Falls, Blue Mountains..." Olivia read off the pamphlet.

"Blue Mountains? That's far; why can't we find somewhere in this parish?" Mia cut in, "We can go to the Martha Brae River, we can go to the beautiful, serene Doctor's Cave beach, We can go...".

"How much did you research, girl?" Chloe interrupted, "I don't think we need a guide; you have everything figured out already! " she added.

Mia chuckled nervously. "Not really. I just like to do my homework about everything".

"So, where should we go first? " Olivia said Mia coyly.

"Leave me alone," Mia answered shyly. "But let's check the house first, though"

"Cool," Olivia intoned.

"Then we rest up after lunch and meet out front for the tour. The house first, then the beaches," Chloe said. "Any other place?" she asked, looking around tentatively.

"Who would have the strength after running around in a house and then going to a beach?" Olivia asked with a dramatic pout.

Mia shrugged. "There are places we could check out tomorrow."

"Cool, we would go with whatever our guide says," Chloe teased.

Avery chewed on her lower lips. "Will there be alcohol?" she asked in a low voice.

The girls laughed; the sound was happy and contented. Chloe took a quick picture and posted it on her Instagram.

'Being surrounded by the best people makes life easier and fun,' she captioned, then put her phone back on the table and refocused on her meal. She planned on eating everything. Food poisoning or not.

CHAPTER TEN

William was silent as Craig drove them to the airport in his pickup truck. They had stopped over at the house to drop off the 'Apology gifts' for Rosie and Stanford Jnr. as they couldn't stay for Thanksgiving. Chloe had been blowing up his phone with pictures, and he couldn't hold off any longer, as the need to be near her was increasing with every breath. The last one she sent of her in a red bikini at the private beach in Negril pushed him to change his flight arrangements and bribe Craig with promises of a good time in Jamaica.

The bikini had exposed her butt cheeks and showed off the dimple on them. Her long-toned legs were draped over the big balloon she was playing with and giving him a view of her flat stomach and perky but full tits. He adjusted his trouser as the thought of her in that position was making him hard. He looked sideways at Craig, who was engrossed on an advert playing on the billboard at the traffic light. William exhaled loudly, thankful that Craig didn't notice the big bulge in his pants.

"Called Mom yet?" Craig asked, breaking the comfortable silence

"Yes. I spoke with Jnr. Too. They sounded thrilled."

" Pamela?" Craig said the unspoken name as a question.

"She wasn't in the room," William replied with a twist of his brows, "thankfully," he added quickly.

Craig nodded and turned up the volume of the radio. Damian Marley's song was playing. "Dude sings just like his brother," Craig said, increasing the volume and moving his head to Damien's

"Medication."

"There's a concert this weekend, the girls are planning on going. You in?" William asked.

"Can't say," Craig said and smirked when William turned to glare at him. "I could be busy with stuff," he added defensively.

" What stuff, Craig. You're a doctor on vacation. Chill out, bro."

Craig shrugged. "How many girls are you talking about?" he asked with a curious glance at William.

"Just five," William said in a monotone, "you should keep your playboy lifestyle away from them, man," William added the last bit as a warning.

"You can't tell me what to do," Craig mumbled with faux annoyance.

William ignored him and brought out his phone to send a quick text to his assistant.

"What if Pamela shows up?" Craig asked after a while.

William didn't say anything for a long minute. Then he shrugged. "She won't," he said, his voice hopeful and pissed. "Mom will make sure she doesn't."

Another song from Damian came up. Craig hit the steering wheel with his right hand. "Damn, he's good," he said, humming the song.

"Yeah. Chloe sent me about two of his songs. She's been listening to Jamaica songs a lot lately," William said, smiling gleefully.

They arrived at the airport thirty minutes before their departure. William wandered off into the mall to get some last-minute items and gum. He saw an image in his peripheral that looked exactly like the lady Craig brought home. He shook it off and proceeded down the deodorant aisle, searching for his cologne.

William found a pendant and a bracelet through the display glass

"How much are those for?" he asked the shop attendant.

"$50000," the man said.

William asked him to pack them for him. He bought a few things and then left the store to find Craig searching for him outside.

"Where the hell have you been, Champ?" Craig asked, his face stamped with worry.

"Was at the store. I'm sorry," William said. He had no idea he was going to stay that long in there. He planned to dash in, get the deodorant, then dash out, but when he found the necklace and bracelet, he couldn't pass them up.

"Come on; we've been waiting for you."

William and Craig walked briskly to the plane as they didn't want to keep the others waiting for much longer.

'I'm on my way, Gem,' he pressed send then settled in the seat that would take him to the woman that made everything in his life near perfection.

* * *

Welcome to Jamaica, where's your luggage, please?" the pot-bellied man said with perfect English. He was their chauffeur. Craig and William showed him their small boxes that were also like a backpack.

"Come on then," he said, after putting them into the trunk of the Bronco. He asked them if they needed music, and William nodded.

William was fascinated by the scenery. The last time he was in Jamaica was when he turned 18, and his parents took him here to watch the Jamaica carnival. He and his family took tons of pictures with Jamaican celebrities that day. Jamaica had changed so much over the years. He could smell the salty beaches air, and the soothing effect he had always experienced came rushing over. For the umpteenth time, he was happy Chloe picked Jamaica.

"Damn, the burning pimento wood is so strong around here," Craig said, sniffing the air like a dog on a hunting spree.

William chuckled. "Rebecca used to love playing outside and taking a stroll on the beach so that she could be closer to the smell even when it was everywhere. Every damn breath".

" I can't wait, Champ; it's thrilling to be here. Chloe made a good one," Craig said, looking around the streets from the car window that was down. "This place is so colorful and ... Damn," Craig said with a twinkle in his eyes. He asked the driver tons of questions about the places.

"You will love your stay here and might even want to relocate," the driver said, smiling brightly.

William saw where he and his parents and Rebecca had a picnic. The Blue Mountains was still as it was years ago. Nothing had changed.

"We are here," the driver said, reversing into a vacant spot in the hotel's parking lot. He opened the trunk and brought out their luggage. "This hotel is the best here," he told them with a smile.

The doorman came down from the steps to take their bags, then directed them to the lobby.

William had booked a separate suite from Chloe, but close to hers - just a few doorways down her hall.

He picked up his key. "I'll see you later, man," he said to Craig.

"At dinner?" Craig asked with a smug grin.

"No, you're going to eat alone, dear. I'm meeting up with Chloe," William said over his shoulders, taking the steps two at a time.

The hotel was calm and a tad chilly due to the beach that wasn't far from the hotel building. Nobody was loitering around, and no unnecessary noise. He smiled and thanked the man when they got to his room. It was a suite, exactly like Chloe's but with a bigger view of the beach and its activities.

William tipped the man then fell face down on the bed. Few hours of sleep, then meet Chloe later. He mused before drifting off to sleep.

CHAPTER ELEVEN

Chloe's mind drifted away from the conversation the girls were having as she stared at William across the bar/restaurant. He made arrangements with the manager for their wedding party the following week. His eyes met hers, and he winked, making her blush evidently. She picked up the glass of water and sipped to avoid the girls noticing her wandering eyes ad red face.

"I'm goin' wear the cowboy boots with glitters," Mia was saying excitedly.

Olivia scoffed, clearly jealous of Mia's choice of dressing.

"Hello Mia," William said, kissing Mia's cheeks briefly, then Olivia, Ava, Avery before he pulled Chloe to her feet and wrapped his arms around her. "I miss you, Babe," he whispered, his eye fixated on hers.

"But you saw me last night at dinner," she purred.

"Not the way I wanted to," he said with mild disappointment in his tone.

Chloe knew what he meant. She had felt the same way, too - tossing and turning in a bed that was too big for her slim body. She had called him to come up to her room, but William, being the gentleman and trying to be the sane one between them, had refused with the promise that in a few days it'd be 'safe' to sleep together and have as much of each other as they wanted. After two hours of discomfort, she had fallen asleep and dreamed about them having sex on a mat by the beach. Her shorts were soaked when she woke up, but she wasn't embarrassed by it. The feeling was good and refreshing.

"Where's Craig?" she asked, trying to change the subject.

"He's somewhere around, doing God knows what," William said matter of fact.

Chloe hit his chest lightly, "Don't be like that, Champ, you have to look out for your friend," she admonished gently.

"Babe..." he pushed her into her seat and leaned down toward her, "what time are y'all leaving for the party?" he asked thoughtfully.

Chloe smirked. "What now, you want to tag along?" she asked, running her fingers down his arms that were placed on either side of her.

"No." William shook his head slowly, his curly hair bobbing around his face. "I want to ask you to come to my room, so we talk after the party." At her raised eyebrows, he smiled vaguely. "Don't be like that, Gem. Our wedding is next week, and we need to talk," he added briskly.

"I see nothing to talk about, Babe," she said, casting him a wry smile, "you just want to feel me," she added with a laugh, drawing the girl's attention.

Mia rolled her eyes at her from the tiny space between Williams's arms. "Pervert," Mia mouthed with a smirk.

Chloe was about to make a snide remark at Mia when William kissed her. "I'll see you later tonight. Have fun, Babe, and text me," he said, then turned to the girls, saluted them, and left to search for Craig.

"You're drooling, Chloe," Olivia quipped.

The girls laughed with Mia pushing a napkin toward Chloe. "Wipe it off, Chloe. It's disgusting to watch," Mia said with a teasing grin.

Chloe blushed harder, the redness spreading down to her chin.

"You sure you won't make him move the date to tomorrow. The heat is unbearable. I can feel it from way over here," Avery chortled but with a serious expression.

"I think so too!" Ava chirped in, pushing her plate away then taking a sip of the water.

"Y'all need to stop being silly." She gasped in apparent dismay at her friend's suggestions, her mind in a tumble.

"You should consider it, Chloe," Ava said gently.

"But before then, we need to get ready for the PARTYYYYYYYY," Olivia said with excitement ringing in her voice

The girls nodded and pushed up from the table.

"We'll meet in Chloe's room in 5, and get ready from there," Avery said; then they all dismissed to their rooms.

***

"Thank heaven it's an open space," Chloe said when they got to the beach and met the massive crowd.

"Damn, it would have been stuffy in a hall or a clubhouse," Ava said.

The girls were lucky enough to find an empty table with just three chairs. So Mia, Ava, and Olivia searched for three extra seats.

"Whoa, be careful," a guy with lips and ear piercings and tattoos on the left side of his face scolded Chloe when she almost bumped into him in her bid to see what was happening around them. She apologized and asked him where the artist was.

"He's on his way, doll," he said, then made to touch her ass, "we could play before the show starts." He winked at her. She scoffed and told him to fuck off. He refused to budge, moving closer to sniff her hair.

"Fuck off, loser!" Olivia bellowed menacingly, with her arms crossed over her chest. The tattoo guy raised his hands in surrender when he noticed she wasn't bluffing.

"I was just playing around," he said in defense. Walking away from them.

Chloe heaved s deep sigh. "Thanks, girls," she said, hugging Olivia than the others. She was in shock. When he had stepped into her space, she didn't know what to do. How to handle him.

"What if he goes around harassing other ladies, even younger girls," she sighed, looking scared.

Chloe just wanted to go back to the suite and cuddle with William. She mentioned this to the girls, but Mia suggested they stay for a few more minutes and, at least, have a peep at the famous artist.

"We came out to celebrate your engagement, Chloe, and we're not going to let some douche bag ruin our night, okay?" she said, looking around at the other girls. They averted their eyes and shrugged. She turned to Chloe, "Say something, babe," Mia persisted gently.

Chloe glanced up from her phone and nodded. "Okay....let's do this."

Ava offered to alert the security personnel while Mia grabbed the drinks.

"Be careful," they said to her, touching her arms gently. She nodded and promised to keep her phone close.

* * *

Mia leaned across the bar, looking around at the others. They were scantily dressed and doused in something she couldn't place. Was it like wood? Grass? She shook her head briskly as if to shake off the scent that was engulfing her.

"Hail up," the barman said. He was dressed in a t-shirt with Damien's picture boldly inscribed. Mia smiled nervously as she was still cautious after what had happened to Chloe.

"Wah gwaan," he said, cleaning the bar top with a rag.

"Hmm.. can I get a soda and a margarita and um, Coke," Mia said slowly in case he didn't understand English.

He shook his head. "We nuh ave dat." He leaned in, towering over her.

"What do you have, please?" she asked politely, trying to rein in her anger.

He smiled and pointed out several bottles on the shelf. The Moscow mule looked delectable, so she picked that and the dirty banana.

"Add rum punch to that tray, Bambi," a deep voice said behind her. She turned to check out who it was and found it hard to close her mouth. He was beautiful in a cowboy-type way and had an enchanting smile that added a soft side to his rather menacing outlook.

"Why's that?" she asked in the most flirtatious tone she could manage.

"You can't say you've been to a party in Jamaica without having the rum punch," he drawled.

She nodded and thanked him, then turned back to the barman. "You heard him."

Beside her was a blonde in a skimpy blue dress and red stiletto heels. She looked pissed and was raving on about a guy that knocked her up, left her and their son to marry another girl in Jamaica. Mia's ears perked up at the mention of a Jamaican wedding. *Could it be William?* she mused, turning to take a closer look at the lady and her two friends. They didn't look familiar, and she didn't remember Chloe mentioning a child in all their conversations. She wanted to tap the woman and ask for the man's name, but how the other glared at her, pointedly told her to back off.

The barman tapped her, his left hand that was placed on the counter. "Your drink ready," he said. His words were sluggish and badly pronounced, but she understood him and picked up the tray with the five glasses of different drinks.

As she turned to go, one of the lady's friends said, "William Stanford ain't getting married to no one." Mia wanted to ask for details, but it would only piss off the girls more, as they looked furious and ready to kill.

Mia walked back to the girls, grateful to be away from the barman that was ogling her tits and the girls that gave her goosebumps with their threats. Were they serious or just really pissed? She sighed and looked around for the girls, as they were no longer where she left them.

"Over here, Mia!" Chloe shouted over the loud music, waving her two hands to get Mia's attention. Mia's heart sunk. She wondered how she would break the news to her dearest friend. She was pulled out of her thought when Chloe rushed up to help her with the disposal tray.

"You okay, Mia?" Chloe asked, looking her over.

"Yeah, just overly excited to meet Damien," she said, faking a smile that didn't quite reach her eyes.

"You sure? This is not your excited look, girl," Ava said, ignoring the cup Chloe was offering to her.

Mia looked away, trying to avoid Chloe's eyes.

"Did the bastard put his hands on you at the bar?" Chloe asked, her words dripping with concern and fear.

Mia shook her head. "No."

Olivia lifted Mia's face with her left hand and peered into her face. "Spit it out. Who did you see?" Then she added with a smug grin. "You have to, so we can all go up there and show off your sexy glittering boots."

Mia exhaled, then grabbed the drink the stranger asked her to get and gulp down the content, wincing as it hit her throat. She made to grab the next when Chloe swiftly handed over the tray to a guy beside them with his friends. "Spill," Chloe commanded her sternly.

"I saw these ladies at the bar," Mia started, looking away from them to the stage where Damien was being introduced. She noticed he was better looking in person and had a charming smile that got the crowd screaming his name. She removed her gaze and focused it on the beach decorated with colored balloons and fancy lights. "They were talking about a man that knocked one of them up and ran off to Jamaica to get married to another woman. They vowed to kill him," Mia gushed out the words, then finally released the breath she was holding.

Chloe let out a low wail, her eyes dilating rapidly. "He can't be him. God no." She leaned on Avery and put her other arms around Olivia. "Did they mention William?" Mia nodded slowly. "Stanford?" Chloe asked again, expecting a no, but Mia nodded the second time confirming her fears.

Chloe pulled out her phone from her purse and typed hastily, her fingers jamming the screen with force. Olivia took the phone from her grasp then pressed send.

"I need to lay down for a while," Chloe said, wiping away the tears that were falling down her cheeks. She was devastated. A big part of her wanted to ask the girls to take her to where William's other woman was, but the need to be in the comfort of her bed and away from the rowdy crowd overcame it. Besides, she didn't want the girls getting into a fight because of her. She smiled ruefully as she recalled the day Avery knocked out a guy that dumped Chloe for a dude in college.

"Can you walk, or should I call a cab?" Ava asked.

" Call a cab," Mia said, removing her boots.

Chloe's phone vibrated with an incoming call. She rejected it and turned on her airplane mood. Tonight, she would cry, then think about her next action tomorrow.

CHAPTER TWELVE

William bellowed a cuss, throwing his phone on the messy bed. Since last night, Chloe had been rejecting his calls, and the girls wouldn't let him see her. They were acting like a fucking shield. Fucking sistahood. "Damn it," he sighed, rubbing his temple. Pamela was so going to get it hard this time. He couldn't believe she followed him all the way to fucking Jamaica to spoil his wedding and cock block him. He picked up the hotel landline and asked to be connected to Chloe's room, but the receptionist told him Chloe wished not to be disturbed by anyone.

Anyone but the girls were with her! He needed to hit something. Someone. Anything. He changed into shorts and a t-shirt. He'd been to the gym just twice in the two weeks he'd been here, so he walked down the wooden staircase to the basements where the gym was located. Craig was there, lifting bars and grunting like a wild pig. William walked past him, ignoring his question about Chloe and the girls as he was unaware of the ground. William had tried calling him, but his phone was not reachable; he had stopped trying after the fifth attempt.

William turned on the treadmill, increasing it to 13km/hr.

He was almost out of breath when someone tapped him from behind. "Hey, you okay, man?" the man that looked to be the gym instructor asked, his lips thinned with worry. William wanted to push his hands away. He needed none of those pity shit.

"I'm fine...thank you," he said instead, then increased the speed limit to a 14.

"You should take it easy on that... It's.."

William turned to scowl at him. "You should mind your own fucking business, Sir," He said the sir with an eye roll before turning back to his workout that was seeping the energy from him gradually.

" Um..." the man started to say again, but Craig pushed him aside gently.

"I'll handle this," Craig said, "thank you." He nodded at the man dismissively.

Craig stopped the treadmill and held the button. "You stink, man. What the hell is wrong with you?"

"You would have found out last night if you had bothered to answer your stupid phone," William gritted out through tight lips.

Craig shrugged. "I was busy, and you asked me not to babysit you."

"It wasn't a babysitting duty," William said grudgingly, leaning against the wall behind him, with his arms folded across his chest. He closed his eyes and said the word that made him want to hurt someone every fucking time. "Pamela."

Craig's eyes widened a fraction in shock and realization. He understood what it meant, even without being told. "But mom said they were together yesterday morning."

"Looks like she left after seeing Rosie," William scoffed in annoyance, "she was at the bar and said something to the girls."

"You sure? I mean, she doesn't even know Chloe." Craig pushed away from the treadmill and trod toward William; leaning on the wall beside him, he touched William's arm. "What did Chloe say?"

William growled deep in his throat. His body vibrated slightly against the wall. "She's been avoiding my calls. Sent Mia to the door last night to chase my ass with a mopping stick."

Craig stifled a laugh. "Mia is the crazy one?"

William nodded. "She almost hit my ass with that shit, man."

Craig nodded apologetically, his eyes filled with worry and fury. He pulled him from the wall. "Come on, let's go get your woman back."

William refused to budge. He told Craig how she sounded on

the voicemail and the text messages, how she wanted nothing to do with him ever again. "She said she's going to enjoy the trip, though, with my credit card," William added with a defeated look. "That means she's not gon' run back to New York immediately. There's a lot to do around here, and I was so looking forward to doing them with her."

Craig patted his back. "Trust me on this, come on."

They walked out of the gym together. Craig tried calling Chloe, but he couldn't, and he decided against sending a voice mail.

They met Olivia on the stairwell. She didn't even bat an eyelash at William.

"That's her friend?" Craig asked, looking behind them at Olivia.

"Yes. You had the chance to meet them the other day, but you were busy chasing Jamaican women," William said, sparing the other man a short glance.

"She's cute."

William stopped, causing Craig to pause beside him. "I told you to stay away."

"You said Mia," Craig argued.

" I said all of them. Five of them," William retorted.

"Okay, but I'll try, though. One of them could be interested, you know."

William ignored him and raised his hand to knock on Chloe's door. After the third knock, a cleaner opened. "Gud Mawnin," he greeted in his thick Patwa accent.

William nodded. "Um, where's the lady that stays here?"

"She go water," he said, "beach."

Craig nodded and thanked him.

William turned to Craig. "We can't go there. She's going to cause a scene."

"Go freshen up. We'll check back later." William jogged down the hallway to his room, pushing the door open, he expected to see Chloe waiting for him, ready to give him a chance to explain instead of calling off their wedding, but the sight he met in there threw him off the edge. He exhaled slowly and walked toward his bed.

"Hello, ladies," he growled, visibly angry.

* * *

Chloe watched him swipe the card over the machine, and it gave her a sense of satisfaction. "Thank you," she said, forcing a smile that didn't reach her eyes. The man didn't notice, though, as he was focused on the zeros being deducted from her account.

"Please come back anytime," the salesman said, handing back her card and the bags with her purchases.

"You make me so proud, girl," Avery said, walking alongside Chloe to the car outside. Mia and others were writing for them in the car. They were famished from the tour to three exotic places on the island.

Chloe laughed, throwing back her head. It was the first real laugh after last night. She was still burdened by it all, but Olivia and the girls found ways of cracking her up, making her forget, which was hard.

She and William had a lot planned. They had so much to look forward to, but now, it was all gone. Sank deep into the Caribbean beaches.

"What did you get?" Ava asked, walking to help carry one of her three bags,

"Shoes for all of you. Bags for Momma, clothes, chocolates, and badass matching swimming trunks for us," Chloe said with an excited grin.

" Go girl!" they chorused, cheering her on.

She winked and flung her hair. "I'm thinking of changing my car," Chloe mused.

"Whatever you want, girl," Mia said, clapping excitedly, "he's a fucking loser," she added angrily.

They got into the car and drove back to the hotel. With Bebe Rexha's "Bad Bitch" blaring from the car radio.

* * *

"Hello, Handsome," the tall one with a lip piercing he didn't notice the day she showed up at his house with Craig cooed. This earned a warning look from Pamela, sprawled on his bed, her long toned legs bared and smooth looking. He removed his eyes and glared at the other girl.

"So you knew who I was?" he asked begrudgingly, flexing his balled fist.

Maya nodded, "I came to check what you were up to. Calvin couldn't stop blabbing about you getting married to a lady in Jamaica," she looked him over, "so, I was curious."

William didn't even care to correct her; he stalked angrily to the side of the bed. "Get out of my bed, Pamela, and take your thugs with you," he growled.

Pamela smirked. "That's not the plan, Willy."

Willy. He wanted to wring her neck.

"Now, here's the thing" she knelt on the bed and ran her fingers down his chest, he didn't move away, "you are going to cancel your wedding, take me back to New York, and marry me as you've always said," she purred.

William removed her fingers slowly from his body. "I don't remember ever saying I'd marry you... now.."

"But she has a child for you," Maya added with a smug grin, "that makes y'all family."

William ignored Maya, focusing his gaze on Pamela. He closed his eyes briefly and exhaled. *God, let me not hurt her*, he prayed in his head.

"How much do you want?" he asked finally.

"A house in uptown Georgia, a nice school for Hanley Jr. and..."

" For fuck sake, Pamela, I got a house for you and my son last year!" he thundered, the veins in his neck popping out.

Pamela shifted away slightly, knowing she was tethering on edge now. "But that's not good enough for us to start a family."

William growled again and walked briskly to the door. "Get out, Pamela," William said, opening the door.

Pamela nodded at the girls and got up from the bed.

"I'll see you around, Willy," she said, making to kiss him, but William moved away quickly.

The other girl winked at him. Maya said something about coming over later.

Fucking idiots!

He banged the door shut and turned to stare at the room, looking over at his disheveled bed.

Who the hell let them in, he mused. He was shaking with fury and hate for Pamela.

He found a pin by the side of the door and bend down to pick it up.

"Fucking Pamela." He turned it over. She had used the pin to unlock his door. It was a trick he taught her when they were dating, and she'd used it on him. Damn it!

He checked his room to see if there were any pictures of Chloe that she might have seen, but none. *That means she has no idea who she is. What if she asks around?* William hit his forehead repeatedly, mutterings curse. This wasn't how he planned this. He had wanted to take Chloe to see his parents' house and take her to all the places he visited with his parents and Rebecca, and now. Damn it!

William hurriedly changed his shirt stained with sweats and pulled a black shirt over his head. Not caring about his shorts, he dashed through the door and ran down the stairs to the lobby. Maybe he'd talk to the manager to keep her mouth shut about Chloe's identity and also tip the staff.

The first person he saw was Craig, talking slowly to a furious Chloe. He had his arms around her and said something funny, William could tell from the way he moved his lips, but Chloe didn't even crack a smile. Was she looking over his shoulder at something? Someone? William couldn't tell, as he was farther away from them and had no view of the other angles except the hotel's front.

William looked around searchingly for the girls. Mia should be there. Olivia too. But there was no sign of the girls. Maybe they went up to their suites. He looked around again, for the manager this time, but the plump woman wasn't anywhere in sight. The staff was busy setting up the place for tonight's Christmas love party. Christmas was next week, but the hotel chose to celebrate a week earlier to allow the patrons time for other festivities on the island. He waved at a man who was arranging the tree. It was big and had all the Jamaican colors, and the bells had beautiful draw-ings on them. Jamaicans were expressive and loved showcasing their arts in various ways. William sighed, his heart beating faster with each breath.

"She's a fucking lunatic!" Chloe's voice swept over him when he was about to head back to his room. He figured he wasn't needed, and she'd probably throw her slippers at him and become more furious. He would ask Craig later, as she had made him promise he'd stay away from her.

"Don't make me hate you, William. Just stay away from me," were her words...he didn't want that. He didn't want to mess up his only chance and force her into leaving. He had transferred ninety thousand dollars into his account when he noticed she had gone shopping with part of the money he had in there. He didn't want her to run out on cash, so he had sent her more. A part of him was hoping she'd call him to rant about sending her money; that way, he'd get to hear her voice. But she didn't. He sighed, his eyes misty with unshed tears. He was going to lose the only person who had given him more reason to live if he didn't act fast. "God, I'm going to get a restraining order against Pamela once this is over," he whispered to himself.

Craig held her tighter when she tried moving away from him toward whatever her anger was directed at. "She's not worth it, Chloe," Craig was saying.

" I don't bloody care, Craig. She had no right to talk shit to me."

"Don't get into a fight now; your wedding is next week, and we can't have you scratching any part of your skin, Chloe."

Since her face was turned in his direction, he could see her facial expression when Craig said they were getting married. She closed her eyes briefly with a pained look. All of this was affecting her; it was draining her. He couldn't wait to make it all go away. All the plans, the promises. God, the sex they were supposed to have in the beach house. His groin tightened like it always did every time he thought about her, the movement making his dick jump slightly; he looked down to check if it was showing through the thin material of the shorts. "Damn," he muttered when he noticed the almost visible bulge.

Chloe made to move again. He was thankful she didn't say anything back to Craig about the wedding. That meant there was a slim chance of her still wanting to marry him. He smiled despite himself.

"You stay away from William, bitch!" a voice that wasn't Chloe's bellowed. Pamela. Shit!

She was she. Who did he think it could be. He chided himself, making to walk down the staircase and beat the hell out of Pamela's body. She was crossing so many fucking boundaries. What the hell was she thinking accosting his woman.

"That's not going to help, Sir," Sheng or whatever her name was, said, stopping him in his tracks.

"What the hell are you talking about," he barked. She didn't flinch. Tough skin. Whatever.

"You look fierce and ready to kill," she said calmly, "Pamela, your ex is aiming for drama, don't give her that, okay?"

William averted his gaze, ignoring her attempt at pacifying him.

"Okay?" she repeated, touching his balled fist. "Go up to your room; I'll send your maid to bring you a bathing oil that will soothe your nerves. Soak in the tub and think about how to get your woman back."

William nodded. Craig was walking toward the entrance now, with Chloe in his arms. She looked spent - visibly tired. He made to rush toward them and take her in his arms. She belonged there, not in Craig's.

"No, she's definitely going to pluck your eyes out if she spots you right now, Sir. Go on up, Chloe is a good woman, and she'll come around. Just.. " she turned to look behind her, then back to him, "play your cards well."

William nodded and turned to go back to his room. He was going to fix this. Whatever it took, he was willing to go all out.

"Bath oil coming right up," Sheng said behind him.

William turned again to see what Craig and Chloe were up to. He noticed her pushing the menu away, definitely not in the mood for food. *That makes two of us, Gem.*

CHAPTER THIRTEEN

Chloe reread the text he had sent the day his ex accosted her in the parking lot and embarrassed her. The text was filled with many emotions: sadness, regret, a need to be near her, and the love in it was glaring at her. She put the phone face down on the bedside table and snuggled into the duvet.

She remembered how he paid attention to every detail and made sure she had everything she needed. She was lucky to have found him. But angry, scared, and hurt that he had a son with another. Why the hell did he not tell her. Was he afraid she wouldn't accept the boy? Was it something she said? Maybe he didn't want her to be involved in that part of his life, but she needed to. The boy was a big part of his life, and she wanted every bit of him. She sighed, leaning her back against the headboard.

Craig had been trying to reach her after that day. He sent her a series of messages and had even sent a delivery man to give her flowers and a bottle of perfume. They were from him and not William. And that bothered her. What if he'd given up and was planning on going back to his baby mama. They had one child together, and a second wasn't bad at all... Damn, she pinched her nose aggressively, trying to let out the anger that was pulsating inside of her. It was directed at him, Pamela, and every fucking thing.

She poured the scotch beside the bed into a glass and gulped it down, wincing slightly at the effect.

Mia and the girls were out touring Jamaica. Today, they were headed to the Frenchman Cove, Blue lagoon, and the park where Sheng said they'd be a crowd and a Christmas festival. She had helped the girls pick out their dresses and walked them to the car before returning to her room to take a nap. Dreams of William canceling their wedding and getting married to his ex made her refuse to go back to sleep. Seeing him in that dream, with Pamela and their son dancing happily, made her stomach churn with anger and resentment. Craig should have let her hit the bitch face when she had the chance.

Did Craig mention the other girl being in William's house? What the hell was she doing there?

Chloe stood up abruptly from the bed, lying there wasn't going to give her answers, and she wasn't ready to face William or Craig yet. She changed into a white sundress, picked up her sunglasses and hat, and walked out of the room. Leaving her insistently ringing phone behind. *William and his best friend can go to hell.* She stepped into the hallway and glanced toward his door, hoping to see him, or worse, Pamela, but there was no one. The hallway was deserted and quiet as usual.

Chloe strolled on the white sand, taking pictures with her camera to later show them to her mom. Karen had no idea about what was going on in Jamaica. She had called the previous night, and Chloe had spoken like everything was peachy. Even when Karen had noticed the sad undertone in her daughter's voice, Chloe had waved her comment off, trying not to embellish it.

The sight of a young boy of about three years old playing in the water with his black parents set her off. She stalked off the beach and headed back to the hotel, waving absentmindedly at the people that were saying hello to her. She was in a sour mood, and it was ruining her day.

Damn, she was never going to get through this shit.

"You okay, Chloe?" Sheng's voice sounded behind her. Chloe wanted to ignore the woman, but she turned and nodded a quick yes.

Sheng smiled. "Want to have a drink with me?" she pushed.

Chloe shook her head. "I'll pass. I'm sorry." she started to walk away. "I just need to lay down for a while," she added hesitantly.

"You've been doing that all morning; your girls left without you," Sheng said, then turned to scold a cleaner that was hovering on the steps. She kept cleaning the same spot for the past 3 minutes. Turning to Chloe, she said, "And for the record, it's Cranberry water, perfect for this weather, don't you think?" she asked with a slow wink.

"I do, Sheng, but no thanks. Another time." She walked off, ignoring the cleaner's greeting. Bitch's ears were at attention, fishing for something to gossip about with others.

"I'll hold you to that, Chloe," Sheng said behind her with a small smile, even when Chloe couldn't see it.

"That's your problem," Chloe wanted to say to her, but the words got stuck in her throat when she saw Pamela leaving William's suite. Alone. Without her minions.

Pamela winked at her and waved. She had the look of someone who had just been fucked. Thoroughly. Her hair was tousled, and her lipstick smeared on her lips, down to her chin.

Bloody hell.

Chloe pushed open the door and banged it shut behind her.

Flowers, in her bed, with a card. Her heart skipped. They were from him; she could tell even before opening it.

She removed the card and opened it, needing to see the bullshit he'd written

Gem...

I'm sorry for every pain I've caused you... I can't...

She tore it into pieces. The asshole was breaking up with her through a damn card and flowers. She ripped up the card and threw flowers against the wall.

The piercing scream that tore from her throat had the floor steward rushing in. He was passing through the door and heard her scream that was muffled due to the soundproof walls but saved on his excellent hearing; he was able to listen to her. He helped her into the bed and asked her who he could call.

"The girls," she mumbled before letting the sobs overtake her.

This was more than she could handle. It was tearing her apart.

She was helpless and totally burdened with hate for a man she once loved.

After calling the girls with her landline, Chloe didn't hear the steward slip out the door.

She was fast asleep before they arrived.

Mia let out a low cuss that sounded like something from a horror movie when she saw Chloe's tear-stained cheeks. She was beyond pissed.

Olivia called the cleaner to clean up the mess on the floor, and then the girls lay beside Chloe on the bed, two on each side. With their arms wrapped around her as best as they could. She struggled in her sleep, moving her head from side to side and mumbling incoherently.

"We're here, Chloe. We're never leaving your side again," Avery whispered, patting Chloe's hair gently.

"Olivia leaned over and kissed Chloe's forehead. "We'll get through this. I promise."

Chloe stopped moving, and her breathing evened. She relaxed into Mia's body that was behind her, snoring softly.

***

"Go out, Chloe. There's a street drama showing today. Go watch it," Ava said.

"The Jamaicans are so fucking talented. They have so much to offer," Olivia added excitedly, hoping Chloe would feel it too.

The girls were trying to convince Chloe to go out. She'd been indoors for the past five days. Her wedding was supposed to be the next day, but it was canceled. She had spent days sobbing and cussing out William.

They hated him too, for what he'd put her through.

"Go on now, Babe. It's something about the birth of Jesus, and you've always loved those churchy things. Go see it and come back before dinner," Mia said, pushing Chloe gently from the bed.

"Okay," Chloe gave in. She brushed her hair and carried her purse with William's card inside. He was yet to ask her to return it. He had even sent some more money into the account yesterday. With a text that read:

'Get everything you need, Gem. I love you so much.'

The nerve of him to want to turn her into a side piece. The nerve of him.

She yanked the door opened and walked through it.

"Keep your phone close," the girls said behind her. She nodded and waved shortly before closing the door.

* * *

After the show on the Jamaican streets, Chloe decided to stop at the store and get a few more things. One of the actors noticed her in the crowd and waved, then turned to tell her friends about the American with skin as clear as a newborn baby. Chloe laughed and told her she was exaggerating. They talked and laughed like old friends. Chloe wished the girls were there to meet her and her friends.

"Enjoying your holiday?" the girl asked in clear English.

" Yes," Chloe replied, smiling nervously.

"What's wrong, you don't look happy?" one of the friends asked, sitting beside her on the bench.

"Oh, nothing, I'm good." She twirled her engagement ring absentmindedly around her finger.

"Bad marriage?" the girl asked.

"No, we were not married yet," Chloe said. It wasn't as hard as she thought. She'd always only had the girls to talk to. Talking to young strangers in the park was new to her, but it was easy. She didn't feel like she was bothering them. They smiled and urged her to continue. So she did. They listened and made no comment until she finished.

"He's a batty hole. A big one," the one with a nose ring said, sounding livid. She swore under her breath.

"What's a batty hole?" Chloe asked, turning to her.

"Asshole," she returned unapologetically. She wanted Chloe to know she wasn't sorry for calling her man an asshole. Chloe got the memo and smiled. "I said so too."

The girls laughed then quietened down after a minute.

"Want us to beat him up for yuh?"

Chloe shook his head. "No, I can handle him. His credit card is doing all the beating he needs," she paused and seemed to be mulling over something, "you girls headed somewhere?" she asked, looking around at everyone to gauge their facial expression. They said no.

"A'ight, come on, let's go shopping," she told them, standing up. They did a fist bump." With his card?"

Chloe smiled; this time, it was a full lip smile, the kind that made her face glow. "Absolutely."

Chloe asked them where she could get Jamaican wear. "Something that will show that I was here, you know," she told the girl.

They took her to a store not far from the park and helped her pick the Kariba suit, bush jackets, and a few bandannas.

She spotted a painting of the country's exotic sights, a tad similar to the one she found in the hotel's restaurant. She picked it and some others.

She was going to gift her customer Jamaican souvenirs. Mrs. Preston would be over the moon with a painting of the beaches.

They were on the last aisle when one of the girl's phones vibrated with an incoming call.

"It's the director," she told the others, and they left hurriedly, hugging her as fast as they could. Another play, and they were to get ready before it started.

"I'll see you around, beautiful one," the girl said, walking out of the store to join her friends.

Then it struck Chloe; she didn't even get their names or phone numbers, no pictures. There was nothing to show the girls except the clothes and paintings and the story they narrated while picking out the clothes. She turned to head to the counter and hit something hard. "What the hell," she muttered angrily, bending to pick up her phone and the painting. Thankfully none was broken.

"I'm sorry, Chloe," Craig said, making to take some of the things from her.

She ignored him and sidestepped to get to the counter. People were beginning to stare, and she didn't want that. Even though they were strangers and would never see her again, she didn't want their noses in her business.

"Look, I'm really sorry, Chloe. Can we talk......"

"Look, save it, okay?" She glared at him angrily. She made her payment and collected the bags.

"Don't follow me, Craig Anderson," she said firmly.

"We need to talk, Chloe. Please."

She whirled around. "He fucking lied to me, Craig!" she thundered. She didn't care anymore. Craig needed to stop being on her ass every damn time. She wanted to forget and move on. And she was almost heading there. Almost.

"He most certainly did not. He just forgot to mention it to you."

"That's still a problem. You can't tell me he forgot he has a son," her voice rang with accusation and anger.

"Let's go to a bar or somewhere to talk, Chloe. Please," he implored.

"Five minutes," she said, stiffly walking toward her car that was parked on the other side of the road.

"We can go in mine, then come back for yours," he said, his voice strained.

"No, I'd rather use mine. I'll meet you at the bar, Craig Anderson," she said, then shot him a scathing glance.

Craig wanted to laugh, but the anger and hurt in her eyes were enough to make him want to mull over in pain. William was becoming a shell of himself. He barely ate and spent his time in the gym hitting stuff, running faster than necessary.

"Okay," he said and got into his car. He waited for her to drive off before reversing into the busy Jamaica streets.

* * *

Chloe sat cross-legged on the sofa facing the beach. She was in the open-air bar, overlooking the water. She averted her glance when she noticed Craig coming toward her, praying silently that William was not with him. She couldn't bear the thought of him with anyone else, and seeing him was going to make her haul him headfirst into the water and let him drown.

Shit, she was turning into an evil witch.

She shook her head to wade off the thought.

She jerked her chin high when she took her seat opposite hers and pretended to be engrossed in a paper plane that was flying overhead.

"Cranberry water," the server said, putting a tall glass of drink in front of her.

She thanked him and pushed the drink away from her to keep her folded arms on the tabletop.

"You have five minutes, Craig. Don't forget that."

Craig sighed and nodded helplessly.

"They met in a party, and after a little back and forth, she agreed to go out with him," Craig started, his voice low and controlled.

"They dated for three years before William found out she was a gold digger and was cheating on him with her boss, so he dumped her." He raised his head slightly to gaze at her.

"I've got nothing to say, Craig. Go on." Her eyes smoldered, and he feared she was going to leave without hearing the whole story.

"I just wanted to be sure you were listening," he told her.

She nodded. " I am."

"She drugged him at a Christmas party organized for his team. How she got in there is something we are yet to figure out," he took a sip of his drink then continued, "after the party, William didn't go home. He had a room reserved in the hotel the party was hosted. He was too drunk to notice her in the room. That night, she had unprotected sex with him unbeknownst to him and got herself pregnant." He took another long sip and tried to gauge her reaction. Nothing. She was tough.

"The following morning, she left before William woke up, and he had no idea, as he was still dressed and all."

She chuckled, disbelief dancing around her eyes. "How did he later find out then?" she asked through a tight smile.

"There were cameras in the hallway, and she was spotted entering his room before him."

She shrugged nonchalantly. "That doesn't explain shit, Craig."

"No, it doesn't. But I think this would." He drained his glass and beckoned to the barman for another.

"William didn't want any part of the child." She scoffed. "My mom had to convince him, and she promised to help take care of him. So, the only thing William did was sign checks and book flight tickets for whenever they needed to go out of the States. He wanted a fresh start, something that would have nothing to do with his past. He wanted to start all over and do it right. With you, Chloe."

"He should have told me," she argued.

"He didn't want to." At her quizzical look, he added. He knew you'd want to be involved in the boy's life, and he doesn't want that, Chloe."

"But they're together now." Her voice was strangled like she didn't want to acknowledge that fact.

Craig shook his head. His face registered shock. "No, she's not even here right now."

She shrugged nonchalantly. "Maybe he's not told you yet. I saw her leaving his room," she said, her voice aloof and reserved.

"Oh, that was when he asked her to come to get the money he knew she was after. She..."

She hit the table with her fist. "Don't bullshit me, Craig. She looked like they had just had sex, and there was no fucking money insight." Her blue eyes stormed as she glared at him.

Craig tried to reach out a hand across the table and hold hers, but she flicked his hands and told him to get out of her sight.

"Please, Chloe. She did try to kiss him. The tousled hair was when he slapped her and kicked her across the room in anger. William was really pissed. He would have killed her if I wasn't there, Chloe. This whole thing is messing him up. He's unstable and has refused to eat or do anything apart from lifting weights and fighting with Jamaican guys." He released a breath he'd been holding and tried reaching out to her hands that were on the table again. This time, she let him take them into his. "You have to do something, Chloe. These guys are tougher, and on hard drugs, they fight bloody. Please."

She nodded wordlessly. "Okay, Craig."

"Okay?" he asked, bewildered. He had expected her to jump up and run to his room. But he figured Chloe was made that way. She was deeply hurt, and all this was taking a toll on her. He looked into her sunken eyes, and his eye nearly teared up. These two people, crazy for each other, were being torn apart. He had wanted to hit Pamela too, but the thought of spending their days in a Jamaican jail superseded that need.

"I need to think this over, and I'll call you with whatever I decide." She stood up to leave. "And oh, tell him to keep the money coming," she added with a smug grin.

He smiled back and nodded. "I will, right away."

She patted his arm and left. Her legs shook slightly as the news of what Pamela did to her man kept replaying in her head. She would tell the girls and then head over to his suite to see him later. She would feed him and nurse him back to the man she'd always known and loved. Pamela wasn't going to win this round. Not again.

CHAPTER FOURTEEN

"We saw the clothes, Babe. Where in the hell did you get them from?" Ava asked the moment Chloe stepped into the room.

Chloe heaved a sigh. "At this store with Jamaican antiques and stuff."

Mia, who was watching a movie on her phone, turned. "What's that look, Chloe?" she asked, her brows furrowing in suspicion.

"Um, y'all need to come closer for this one," Chloe said; sitting on the bed, she clamped her hands on her hips.

"Come out, Ava, you can shit later!" Olivia called out to Ava, who was in the toilet.

The girls snickered. "You say it like poop can be paused," Mia said between laughter.

"She's been in there for hours," Avery quipped.

"Probably using her vibrator," Olivia added, her lips quirking upward in a knowing smile.

"Something you not telling us, Liv?" Mia asked, her gaze flickering to the other girl.

"No, Mia. She's just sputtering nonsense as usual," Ava said, coming into the room. "I heard everything," she told them, then her gaze settled on Chloe, "but that can wait. I'll chew y'all asses later. What's wrong, Babe?" she asked Chloe solemnly.

Chloe shook her head gently in a gesture of unease. "Craig."

"William's Craig?" Olivia asked.

Chloe nodded.

"I've never met the guy, but if he's said anything to hurt you, I'll have his ass in a burning flame," Mia seethed.

Chloe released a long sigh. She was expecting this. They'd be mad, but she hoped to God they'd understand too. She needed them too. All this had been too much, and she missed William. The island would soon be flooding with people, and the plan was to have a quiet wedding in a calm environment. That wouldn't be possible with the crowd around. She needed to fix it, so they could all have fun and head back to their lives in New York.

"Spill, Chloe. I'm losing it," Olivia said tightly.

She did. Starting from when she met the girls, the scene at the store, and the bar conversation.

Mia was out the door before she could even say the final words.

"Mia!" she screamed and ran after Mia. But was too late, as she was already down the stairs. Not William then, Chloe realized, turning back to the room.

"Where's she headed?" Olivia asked...her voice reserved.

"Probably to the bar to get us drinks," Chloe said.

"I doubt it. That wasn't a going-to-get-drinks look, girls," Ava said, a frown knitting her forehead. "Where's Craig's room?"

Craig! Chloe realized that Ava was right. Mia was after Craig.

"Let me call the front desk," Chloe said and picked up the phone.

Damn it, and Mia was going to onslaught her anger on the poor guy. He did nothing wrong, or maybe he did? Chloe frowned at the thought. He should have told her since William refused to.

"It's on the third floor!" she announced.

The girls nodded but didn't budge from their positions on the bed.

"Come on, girls, let's go get her." Chloe stared at them in surprise.

Olivia picked up her phone and opened her Instagram. Ava connected her phone to her speakers, Avery was stifling a laugh.

"Chill, Chloe. Those men deserve it. I wish it were William, though," Olivia said, her eyes burning with fury.

Damn, the girls are at it again. She mused and walked over to the door.

"Don't," they thundered when she made to turn the knob. "Sit down, Chloe. Do you need something to eat? Drink? Should I order room service?" Ava asked, smiling benignly.

"No, I'm fine," Chloe said, coming over to sit on the couch.

"Good." Avery nodded and patted her hands gently. "We'll handle it later."

Later. That's going to be after they've known that Mia has finished lashing out at Craig. Shit. This was bad. She made to grab her phone and call the manager to check on Craig.

"No, that is not acceptable, Chloe," Olivia said, shaking her head with a knowing grin. "Don't make me lock you in your own bathroom, girl. You're disturbing my mediation," she added with a wry grin.

Chloe moved to the couch beside the window and started counting from 100 backward. Her eyes closed tightly. She didn't want to think about Mia's last time to "handle" someone. Aaron was Ava's manager at the bar in college and had tried putting his hands in Ava's dress one night. The girls were in the bar where they had gone to wait for Ava to finish her shift, so they'd all head out to the club when they heard a shriek and cussed loudly. Before anyone could react, Mia was out of her chair and heading toward the sound. They got in there two seconds later to find the pot-bellied man sprawled on the floor and unconscious.

"I'm thinking about it too, Chloe," Ava said beside her, "and this time, it's going to be worth it too."

Chloe opened her eyes to stare at Ava. "But Craig isn't at fault," she argued indignantly.

"They're friends. Birds of the same feather, shit," Olivia intoned.

* * *

"You had the nerve to fill her head with nonsense," Mia seethed, towering above Craig, who was seated on the couch

"You should have fucking stayed away, Craig. What your friend did is no way excusable, and you know that!"

He turned to tell her that William was suffering too, but the pure anger he saw in her eyes had him swallowing his words.

She kicked the table, demanding that he look at her while she was talking. "You are going to be all bloody if you don't stop stalking my girl," she said tersely.

This must be Mia, the one William said is fierce. She really was, but her body spoke differently; the curves in all the right places and her face bare of makeup was alluring. He chided himself for having carnal thoughts about a woman that was only set to tear him limb from limb.

"You shouldn't be here, Mia," he said her name out loud, the sound of it making his ears tingle. "I had to tell Chloe William's reasons for holding out.. they are.."

"No, you didn't do that. You made excuses for him. You both are cowards, and I'd love to slap that stupid smirk off your awful face." She made to grab him, but he dodged. He knew she was going to, so he had prepared himself for the attack

"Calm down, Mia.. please... Just."

"Don't fucking tell me to calm down!" She glowered. "Y'all are just going to hurt my friend and toy with her emotions, and I don't want that shit."

"He's not going to…he's miserable without her. You need to…" he said in a voice her mama used whenever she was trying to coax her into doing something bad. Her annoyance grew, and she made to grab him again.

"By God, if you dare tell me to calm down again, I'm going to have your limbs," she bellowed, pointing her fingers at him.

"I wasn't going to do that. I just need you to.."

She cut in again, and he realized how much fury she was harboring this time. It wasn't just aimed at him, but at William too. He found her outburst a little over the top and made to leave the room. She kicked the table, sending the contents all over the floor. When she grabbed his shirt, the door burst open, and the girls rushed in. Chloe held her back, whispering incoherently into her ears. Craig stormed out of the room, ignoring the girls and Chloe's attempt at pacifying him.

"Damn, she was almost there. I told you all we should wait a bit," Olivia said.

"His face is still looking pretty," Ava added, glaring at his back.

"Come on, Mia, let's go," Chloe said, leading her away...

He went back after they'd left and arranged the table. He wondered how William was going to cope with all that drama. Where the hell was he going to fit in, he thought wearily.

* * *

"That was uncalled-for, Mia. You shouldn't have attacked him. He was..." Chloe said with an edge to her voice.

"Don't, Chloe.. fucking don't," Mia retorted, cutting Chloe off.

The girls were back in the room after lunch, and Chloe tried to get Mia to apologize to Craig. He was just a middleman and nothing more...she was wrong to have lashed out at him like that.

"He's his fucking best friend, and he tried to make you get back with William!"

"I'm going to get back with William, Mia. Craig explained everything to me, and I told you guys too. He is wrong, but it's nothing we can't work on. Please Mia," Chloe said imploringly. Holding the girl's hand.

"Okay, I will," Mia said with an eye roll, "but first, I need to sleep; I'm tired." She pushed Ava's feet away to lay beside Olivia.

"All that shouting is sure to make one tired," Avery quipped.

"Well done, Mia. He was visibly pissed. I wanted to laugh in his face," Olivia said, giving Mia a high five, which the other returned with a smug grin.

CHAPTER FIFTEEN

They were on the hotel's balcony having breakfast when Craig spotted them. He was in his gym gear and heading toward the stairwell when Olivia waved at him. He paused, his face registering surprise.

"Come on, Craig, the girls, are harmless," Chloe said, smiling widely.

"You make it sound like we're dogs, girl," Mia chided.

" Ain't you," Chloe whispered under her breath.

"Bitch!" Mia said, then picked up her glass to take a long sip when she noticed Craig was a few feet away from them. She had gone to his room to apologize last night. He was shirtless and refused to put one on even after noticing her glares.

He had smirked and told her to avoid balconies. That was when it clicked - he was the man that night on the patio.

Craig found himself wanting to see more of the spark of challenge and fury in her gaze. He liked the fierce woman who spurted words of anger at him. He felt himself growing hard at the thought of her under him. She was out the door before he even told her she'd been forgiven. He had chuckled, totally convinced that the girls or Chloe roped her into doing it. But it was worth it; the fire was still there, just slightly dimmed.

"Hello, ladies," he greeted, bending down to accept Chloe's cheek.

"Hey, Craig. You okay?" Olivia quipped with a playful grin.

"Of course, why wouldn't I be?" he asked, feigning ignorance.

"Our girl did a number on you, didn't she?"

"Oh," he chuckled and turned to Mia, "she apologized, so it's water under the bridge now," he added with a wink.

"Too cocky, it's suffocating," Mia said, waving her hands dismissively.

"You're so cute, Mia," Craig said.

He noticed the hiking glare. "Going hiking?" Chloe nodded. "You should come along, Craig," she added. Mia kicked her shin under the table. "Ouch, don't be like that, Mia. We need a chaperone."

Craig smiled. "I'll come. Let me shower quickly and meet you, ladies, back here."

"Had breakfast?" Ava asked.

"No, Mia will pack a bite for me," he said with a wry grin. Mia snorted and ignored him.

"She definitely will," Chloe assured him, "see you later, Craig."

Chloe could see the question in his eyes. He wanted to know if she'd spoken to William. She shook her head. "Tonight," she mouthed. He nodded and smiled with satisfaction.

* * *

"Go, Mia, take the food to him," Chloe said gently.

"I will, Chloe. Stop pushing it."

Chloe walked away to join the others. Someone was passing out coffee. The mountain was famous for its coffee, and she heard from a lady who was also here for a holiday that it was better than New York's coffee.

The hike was exhilarating. She had used that time to think and decide what she would say to William.

She turned to see Mia heading toward Craig. He was watching her under his hooded gaze.

"Hey, Chloe, come on, let's hike to the other side and take a dip in the chilly water," Ava said, pulling her toward the others. William would have loved this. She looked at her phone, expecting a text or a missed call. There was nothing. She put it back and ran to meet Ava's long strides. She'd meet with William later; right now, she was going to make memories with her girls and watch Craig and Mia flirt with each other.

* * *

Craig watched as a bead of sweat trickled down the valley between her breast and wanted to reach out and brush it off with his fingers.

"Thank you for looking out for us; that was brave," she said. He had stepped in to hold Avery when she slid down the steep mountain. How he was able to do, that was something she found awe-inspiring.

"Was that enough to earn a dinner date?" he asked.

She shrugged. "Yeah. I'd love that. You've saved me twice."

"Twice?" he asked, acting coy.

"Yeah, at a party in New York and here with the girls. So, yes, let's do dinner," she beamed at him. The sight of it made him want to capture her face. She was beautiful, with her red hair packed into a ponytail and high cheekbones, giving her an enchanting look.

"Thanks, I'll pick you up at 8 pm." He paused and looked at her, taking her all in. She blushed, and damn, it was refreshing to see. "And, um," he cleared his throat, "thanks for the food, I appreciate it."

She nodded and waved him off. "I'll see you later, Craig," she sashayed away after they'd exchanged contacts.

"Damn," Craig muttered under his breath before adjusting his shorts to contain the bulge.

CHAPTER SIXTEEN

Chloe sprawled lazily on the couch in the sitting room, reading a book while also listening to Mia's gist about Craig to the other girls. Chloe smiled at her friend's boldness, but she wished she could see William but her friends have the guarding the door all night, preventing her from going out.

A knock on the door made Chloe sit up straighter, hoping it would be William. Ava stood up to open it; she had missed him.

"Oh, hi, Craig," she cooed with a playful grin.

Mia blushed, the redness spreading down her neck. Chloe snickered. "Hello, Craig."

Craig nodded a greeting and went over to sit by Mia, who was still tongue-tied. He handed her the flower and chocolate he had brought for her.

Mia brought her nose to the flowers and smelled them. "It smells nice, thank you" She blushed.

"Did you sleep well?" he asked her quietly. She nodded.

"She did. You know that, Craig," Chloe said with a short laugh. Craig chuckled, oblivious to the girls' banter.

Chloe stood up and picked up the flowers he had brought for Mia. "I'll find a vase for this, Mia. And your chocolates are going to the orphanage."

Craig stopped her. "Stay, please." She gave him a surprised look. "I need to talk to y'all about something," he said pleadingly. She nodded and beckoned the girls to join them on the couch.

Craig heaved a deep sigh. "It's about William." He looked around to see if any of them had an issue with what he was about to say. He continued when he got no reaction. "He's made plans to fly Hanley in so that y'all can meet him, and ... he's really sorry."

They said nothing and just stared blankly at him. He sighed, looking defeated. "Um, I'll see you guys around." He stood up to leave.

"When is the boy coming in?" Chloe finally managed to say.

"Tomorrow morning," Craig replied.

They nodded again. Mia thanked him for the flowers and chocolates.

"You're welcome, Mia." And he was out.

Chloe crossed her arms across her chest and stared at the bright sky devoid of clouds outside the window.

"Can I go see him now?" she asked.

The girls pretended not to hear her, then. "No, you'll see him tomorrow. Come on, let's go for the parade; I heard there would be fireworks," Mia said, opening the wardrobe.

* * *

William returned the phone to its cradle. "They're here," he said to Craig.

Craig nodded absentmindedly.

"What is it, Craig?" he asked in a strangled voice.

"I hope this works," Craig said with a forlorn look.

" I hope so, too," William whispered and sent a silent prayer to God...he was tired. Being without Chloe for the past few weeks showed him how much he needed her. Everything became meaningless when she told him to stop bothering her life.

He'd been stalking her and the girls. The day they went to the Blue Mountain, he was there in the small crowd, hiding behind a hoodie he picked up from the hotel mall. He had seen her eyes searching around more than three times like she was expecting to see someone in the crowd. His heart nearly jumped out of his body when she almost slipped on their way up. He smiled a sad one when he noticed Craig stepping in to help her. That should have been him. That night, he had gotten drunk and fallen asleep in his own vomit until Craig found him the next morning and had helped clean him up.

"Gotten everything," Craig's voice sounded from the sitting room.

"Yes!" he shouted back as best as he could so Craig could hear him.

Chloe stepped outside her room with the girls in tow when he closed the door behind Craig and him. She smiled and waved. It was heartbreaking to see her and not touch her. He nodded and looked beyond her to the girls that were behind her. They weren't glaring at him, which was a relief, but they weren't smiling either.

They took the elevator. So, William turned to Craig. "Let's use the stairs." Craig nodded wordlessly and followed his best friend to the stairs.

Hanley was standing with Helena, William's cleaner, when they got down to the lobby. Rosie couldn't make the trip as she was still recovering from an illness.

William scooped the tall five-year-old in his arms and kissed his forehead. Turning to Helena, he welcomed her and thanked her for bringing Stanford. "It's no problem at all, William," Helena said, understanding evident in her blue eyes.

"Come on, pal. There's someone I'd like you to meet," William said, taking the boy's hand in his and walking toward the girls.

Chloe bent down to hug him. She sniffed his hair and smiled. "You're so beautiful, Stanford. I can't believe your father kept you away from him."

"Thank you, Ma'am," Stanford said shyly.

William came over and knelt beside him. "Stanford, this is Chloe, the woman I want to get married to," he said slowly.

"She's gorgeous and doesn't look as mean like my mom," he said to his father, but Chloe could hear him. She smiled and ruffled his hair before standing up from her crouched position on the floor.

William held her right hand when she made it to walk back to the girls. "Dinner tonight, please, Chloe." He reveled in the feel of his skin touching hers after a long while.

"Say yes, Ma'am," Stanford pleaded when he noticed that Chloe wasn't saying anything.

Chloe looked down at him and smiled. "Yes," she said to William, but her eyes were fixed on his son, "and, you can call me Chloe."

Stanford nodded and clapped excitedly.

The girls went over to talk to Stanford. They all ignored William except Mia, who was subtly flirting with Craig. After that first night, they had made it a routine. The sex was great, and he kept raising the bar, making her want him more and more. He was like a soothing balm, kneading her kinks and helping her relax her nerves.

"Can I talk to you for a second, please?" William asked. His gaze settled on the four girls.

"No," they said in unison.

"Go talk to her, William, and make it right this time," Olivia added.

"Everything okay, Dad?" Stanford asked, glancing up at his father.

"Soon, soon, very soon," he said, looking over at Chloe. Their eyes met, and she averted her gaze, but not after sending him a warm smile. His heart warmed with love, and he found his strength seeping back into his bones. He felt alive after so many days of being gloomy.

***

The car drove slowly down the streets of Jamaica. William was taking them to his family's villa in the City. Chloe was beside him in the front seat, her hands clasped in his as he sang along to a Jamaican song that was blaring from the car radio. He told her he had spent most part if his days that they were apart learning Jamaica music. He could sing a few and speak the language a tad fluently.

They arrived at the villa, with Craig's car trailing behind them, and parked on the empty spot beside William's car. Mia's hair was tousled, and her lipstick smeared the moment she stepped out of the car. Chloe laughed and pointed it out to Ava, who nudged Avery, and before Mia could know what was happening, the girls were laughing and shaking their heads at her.

Craig and William were busy checking the surrounding. There was a car in the driveway, a sign that there were new occupants of the house he had loved as a child. That saddened him. He wondered if they were taking good care of the garden his mother started back. He raised his balled fist and knocked twice, then stood against the railing when he heard footsteps coming from inside the house. A woman in her late forties opened the door and smiled at them.

"How can I help you, please?" she asked, blocking the doorway with her thin body.

"Um, this is my parents' house and ..."

The woman's eyes lit up immediately with recognition.."Ohh, you're William Hanley?"

William nodded, pleased that he didn't have to explain himself further.

"You have so grown and very different from the pictures we've seen," she opened the door wider, "please come on in."

William waved the girls over, and they trod into the house. It was still the same, and the only difference was the furniture and the dining set.

He glanced around at the familiar yet strange space. He saw a family portrait hanging by the fireplace and took in the family of three. The woman and probably her husband was sitting on a couch, and three teenage girls were beside them. *If she is married, then where is her husband?* He mused.

"Offer them drinks, darling, don't stand there staring," a man's voice sounded behind them. He came into view. He was short and had on a shirt with Jamaica's drawings.

"Welcome," he said and settled into the rocking chair that was facing the doorway.

William and the others greeted him. "How are you, Sir?" William asked politely.

"I'm very well, son." He lifted his legs onto the center table. "Who are you?" he asked not too politely.

William explained himself and watched his face contort with anger. That was unexpected, as he didn't even know the man

"Where the hell have you been all these years. We packed your parent's things into the basement, and I've been expecting you to come to take them out. I need that place to be used as an office," he said hurriedly, his tobacco-stained lips cracked, making his words sound forced and sluggish.

"We will go get them right away, Sir," William answered, his tone slightly pissed.

"You do that, boy."

William led Craig and the girls to the basement.

"Sit in a corner, and we'll handle this just fine," Craig said to William and Chloe.

"Why?" Chloe asked abruptly.

"You're getting married tomorrow...we don't want you stressing yourselves. Just go," Mia said, shooing them out of the dusty room. Everything was packed into boxes and piled up into the two cars within the next hour. William had cried when he saw his father's clothes packed into a torn, dirty box. He felt guilty for not coming earlier.

It was beginning to get dark when they drove out of the villa. The woman waved, telling him to stop by again before traveling back to the States. Like hell, he would.

"I'm sorry," Chloe whispered, kissing him softly... it was their first kiss after they made up two days ago. He kissed her back, his mouth lingering on hers, and he returned it vigorously.

"Take it easy, guys," Mia said when she saw them.

"You're not one to talk, Mia. You should stop bothering with lipstick. It gets smeared all over your face every time you use it," Ava said with a mischievous glint. Mia told them to stop monitoring her.

"We're not. You're just in our faces every time, girl."

The ride back to the hotel was slow, as the streets were filled with people.

"It's going to get real noisy around here now," Chloe said.

William turned to her. "We'll be married tomorrow, and all this will be over."

"But I don't want it to be." She pouted.

"Then we can stay, extend it again."

She nodded and leaned over the window to watch the people dance in the streets. It was colorful and exciting to watch.

* * *

Craig kissed Mia again and pulled her into his arms. "Want to continue this when we get back to New York?" he asked her lightly.

She shrugged. "I'd love to. I mean, you have a great body, and I'm yet to get enough of it. So, yeah," she threw him a teasing grin and kissed his Adam's apple, "you are naked," she purred and massaged his balls, her fingers wrapping gently around his dick.

Craig moaned and trailed his fingers along her stomach, teasing her senses. Mia took him into her mouth and sucked slowly, her tongue swiping over the head of his dick before she swallowed him again, making gagging sounds.

Craig pulled her up swiftly. "If you continue that, we're going to stay here longer than we have to," he breathed. His eyes were dark, and she could see him trying to control himself. She didn't want that. Mia wanted him to be wild and free with her. Yes, it was just sex, but they could learn to please each other without holding anything back.

She pulled her body away from his grasp and stared into his eyes that were dark with passion and so much lust. "The wedding is not until 4 pm; come on, Craig. Make me beg again."

He drew his mouth down her neck, sending shivers of pure craving and a need to be possessed down her body. She jerked atop him, her soaked underwear drilling on his belly.

He stared at her for a moment before turning them around. "It's going to be fast and rough, Mia," he whispered.

Heat flushed her cheeks, and she nodded. "Just fuck me already, Craig."

He pushed into her, his muscles pulsating with the force he used. She screamed out in pain at first before her pussy adjusted to take him all in, moving her hips to meet his thrusts, her eyes rolling with pleasure.

***

"I now pronounce you husband and wife," the clergyman said,

smiling widely at them.

William's expression eased at once, a weight lifted from his shoulders, and he wrapped his fingers around her before lifting up her face to meet his in a kiss that would bind them together forever. Chloe smiled into his mouth, her eyes misty with unshed tears.

"Husband," she said, grinning with pleasure.

William laughed and turned them to meet their friends and a few people from the resort.

The wedding was on a private beach. William had booked the space and a room for their honeymoon.

Chloe waved at the girls and beckoned them to come to her. She noticed the girls she met at the play that day, and her smile grew wider. "They came," she gushed happily.

"Congratulations, Chloe, William," Ava said, hugging them both.

"Better not fuck this up, or I'll fuck up your face, army god," Mia warned. *How very prompt*, William thought.

"The only thing you seem to be fucking right now is Craig," Olivia said in a mock whisper, "where is he, by the way?" she asked, turning to William. "Don't pretend you didn't hear that, Willy," Olivia mimicked Pamela. "You're going to be hearing a lot of shitty talks now that you're married to the queen."

William cast her an exuberant grin and nodded. "I look forward to all of it," he said, brushing his lips against Chloe's, "let me go say hi to our guests. I'll see you in a short while." He strode away, Chloe's smile of obvious delight was contagious, and the girls smiled back, visibly happy for her.

"Hello, bride," the first girl said.

Chloe rushed and hugged them. Her wedding dress from Anne Berge fluffing around her like a sea of water.

"I'm so glad you came." She hugged them and asked for their names. They told her their English names, as they didn't want to stress her with their Jamaican names.

"Come on, Chloe, let's take a group picture for the gram," Mia said, dragging her away from the girls. " I'm sorry, girls, she'll be back," she apologized over her shoulder.

Chloe stood in between the girls; they were clad in blue maxi beach dresses with red heels and hats to match.

"You're glowing, Babe. I'm so proud of you," Ava said, patting Chloe's hand affectionately.

"We're all proud of you," the girls said.

She was too. After everything they'd been through, William and she were able to pull through it all, unscathed. She searched for him in the crowd, and when his eyes met hers, she smiled and blew him a kiss. At that moment, the camera flashed, capturing the pure love that was oozing from every part of her body.

* * *

The music was soft and seductive. It matched their mood as they stood at the center of the room, wrapped in each other's arms. Still, in her dress and 6-inch heels, Chloe pulled his head down a little to meet her lips. She savored the taste of him - he tasted like grapes and lime. She trailed her lips down the side of his mouth, biting, soothing, craving more. She wanted to leave her marks all over his body, as it wasn't just sex for her - this was the start of a life that was going to be filled with so much bliss and love. She unbuttoned his shirt and pulled it slowly down his arms. The workout had changed him, she noted with a tiny smile. His muscles were more visible, and his nipples were taut. She ran her tongue over the tightened knobs and sucked on them gently, increasing her speed as his body spasmed with the feel of her tongue on his body.

Chloe trailed her tongue down to his belly button, sucking gently in the hole that was there before moving to the V that led to his groin. William muttered a curse, his breathing heavy and rushed, his eyes glued on her every move. She removed his belt and unbuttoned his pants, pulling it down first before his underwear.

His dick came into view, and she swallowed, her throat dry with wanting. She had seen him before, but she had also forgotten how he looked. He was big, intimidating, and she felt hungry for him anew.

She couldn't understand how she had stayed away from him for this long. She ran her fingers over his full length, and he moaned.

"Don't do that," he growled, pulling her up. His eyes had turned a shade darker, or was it blue, she couldn't tell, as her eyes were glossed over with need and the crazy longing to be made love to by him. "I will please your body like it is the first time."

"Every time with you is like my first time," Chloe whispers breathlessly.

William turned her around and unzipped her wedding dress, trailing his tongue down her back and biting every spot visible to him.

He threw the dress on the couch in the room and turned her to face him. "I Love you so much, Chloe," he whispered with contentment.

She wanted his touch, arching her back to present her perky but full tits to him. He worshipped them, his tongue and lips swiping slowly like he was tasting his favorite dish for the first time. He was, and he wanted to make it memorable. He wanted to revel in her and make her scream his name over and over again.

William carried her to the bed after he'd removed every piece of clothing from her body except her heels.

He pushed up the pillows and rested her head gently on them.

William turned out the lights except for the bedside lamp. He wanted to see her, every inch of her. I wanted to see the way her body responded to his touch. The pure bliss of being here like this with her was exquisite.

William spread her legs and inserted a finger into her cunt, the wetness soaking his fingers.

He licked it off and inserted it again. This time he curved it gently, his eyes glued on hers as he fucked her with his fingers. She moaned, writhing on the bed. He increased the tempo and watched her close her eyes tightly, her lips apart, her nipples begging for his touch.

"Look at me, gem," he commanded slowly. She did. He took her; she gasped, loving the feel of his breath against her skin...

William spread her legs farther apart and got between them. He turned his dick on her cunt, once, twice, then pushed in gently. He groaned from the warmth of her, moving slightly to get used to the feel of him in her tight cunt.

He moved forward and crushed her lips with his. She kissed him back hungrily with a passion that was so intense; he found himself growing harder. Her scent filled his nostrils, and he breathed it in. His hips moved slowly to please them.

It wasn't rushed but slow, deep, and mind-blowing.

CHAPTER SEVENTEEN

The girls were back in New York. Chloe was set to meet with the secretary for a meeting concerning the Christmas party that was to take place the following day. She had returned to complete several missed calls and messages on her answering machine. Her assistant was able to handle Mrs. Preston's dress and some others, but the poor girl could not deal with most of the demands made by the clients. She was at Mia's. William had traveled on a mission, and there was no way she would stay in that big house of his alone. The moment he left, she had packed a bag and a few necessities to stay with Mia, as the others were preoccupied with stuff unknown to her.

Mia was sprawled on the couch with the remote and a box of tissue. She had been in that position for the past hours. Her eyes were glued to the TV, and her body was covered with the thick blanket from the guest room.

"You sure you'll be okay, Babe?" Chloe asked for the umpteenth time that morning.

"It's just the flu, Chloe. I'm not bedridden," Mia retorted in a croaky voice.

"You sure? You've been in that position for the past 5 hours."

"It's the med. The lady said I should rest after taking it. That's the only way it's going to work."

Chloe nodded and muttered an okay before leaving the room. She would call the girls and have them take Mia to the hospital. There was no way she'd be able to stand against three lofty women. No way.

* * *

"What's in the pack?" Olivia asked Ava, who was sniffing a pack of alcohol she'd found on the floor beside Mia.

"Smells like alcohol."

"It can't be," Avery said with a hint of disbelief in her voice, "who takes alcohol for flu?"

"That's John Crow Batty; it works for flu too," Mia said groggily, raising her head slightly to glare at the girls. "And keep your voices down, bitches, my head hurts."

"It's going to hurt more if you don't stand up this minute and get dressed so we can drag your ass to the hospital," Olivia said, a threat ringing in her voice.

"But I'll be fine. It's just the flu," Mia argued, snuggling deeper into the pillows.

"Let Dr. Sharon tell you that, girl. Get your ass up." Ava said her words short and clipped.

"Okay. It's just the hospital, not a death sentence. Stand. Up," Avery added in a stern voice.

Mia scoffed. "Y'all should be treating me nicely. I'm sick, you know."

"You don't do nicely. This is the only way to get you to stand up," Olivia pointed out, removing the covers from Mia's body.

The hospital was busy, and people were crying in the hallway as there was news of an accident on fifth avenue that morning. Mia didn't have to join the queue, as she was a special patient of Sharon's.

She stepped into the doctor's office and sat down without invitation, her eyes puffy and the light streaming into them, making her squirm.

"This should be quick, Doc. It's just the flu, and I need something to take for it," Mia said the moment she sat down, ignoring the other woman's attempt at pleasantries.

Sharon smiled. Mia was one of her most troublesome patients, but Sharon admired her spunk. "You can't know that," Mia rolled her eyes, "okay, what are the symptoms you've been having?"

Mia listed them off with her fingers and then shrugged. "It's the flu."

"Let's take a test to be certain, okay?"

Mia nodded as she had no strength left to argue.

The doctor returned with the result and a smile that set Mia off an hour later. "What are you so happy about, Sharon?"

"Go ahead, open it."

Mia opened the paper and what she saw was in no way good news. She stood up slowly and walked out of the room without a word.

"You okay? What did she say is the problem?" Olivia asked, her face stamped with worry.

Mia muttered one word, and they nodded silently.

There was no way she was going to break the news in a damn hospital and have the girls blow her up with questions. She knew it was Craig's, as she had not been with another for a long time after and before she met him. Rico was just a crush and nothing else, so it was solely Craig's. She would tell the girls; they would help her figure out her next course of action.

When they arrived at her house, Chloe's car was parked in the driveway. Mia released a sigh, partly happy she wouldn't have to repeat the news. All the girls were here.

"Come on, I can smell muffins and meatloaf sandwiches," Ava said, taking the steps two at a time. She opened the door and held it for the others to go through before closing it.

Chloe came out from the kitchen when she heard their voices. "How did it go?" she asked, wiping her hands on the towel she was holding.

"I'm pregnant," Mia announced and sat down heavily on the couch. She was both devastated and happy. Devastated because she and Craig agreed to just sex with nothing attached, now a baby was going to change all of that, and she wasn't sure how he'd react.

Happy because she was carrying something they created together on their last day in Jamaica. She knew it was from the night he took her against the wall. That night, she saw the stars and danced with the angels. She smiled and rubbed her belly. "It's

Craig's," she whispered the words, but the girls heard her as their attention was glued on her, waiting to listen to her next words.

"I have his address," Chloe said excitedly, "I found it when I was cleaning out the bag you traveled with.

Mia didn't remember taking his address. He had agreed to visit twice a month. Maybe he must have slipped it in there.

"Come on, let's pack you a bag," Olivia said, dragging Mia from the couch, "you're going to look for him, girl. You can't do this alone."

Mia nodded and followed her friends into her room. She definitely couldn't do this alone. She would have the girls, yes. But she would need a man's assistance too.

It means the world to me that you brought my book. Writing is my passion and I look forward to hearing from you.

So if you liked this book, I'd like to ask for a small favor. Would you be so kind to leave a review on Amazon? It'd be very much appreciated!

Misty Rosette

p.s. A review is like a warm hug to us authors – we love it!

Love in London (Love and Travel Series Book 4)

She knew it was a quick fling. Then why can't she get him out of her head?

My life is about to turn upside-down, and I can't hide it anymore. I know I have to find Craig and tell him the truth.

There's one big problem – I don't know where Craig lives.

And when my girlfriends and I finally manage to track him down, things don't go according to plan… at all.

My relationship with Craig started as nothing more than a quick fling. Now things are getting all-too-real, and I don't know if my emotions are going to get the better of me.

As I struggle to work things out with Craig, my best friend Avery finds herself caught up on a date with Craig's rich and successful boss. She swears she's not interested in him, but I can sense something much more budding beneath the surface.

Avery can have any man she wants. Will she fall for the unlikeliest of suitors? And can I convince Craig that we were meant to be together?

ABOUT THE AUTHOR

I am a hopeless romantic. Since childhood, I have always been interested in romantic tv series, novels, shows, etc. Also, I have been an avid reader since the age of 3. When everyone around me was busy playing, my comfort space had always been in books. When I was a teenager, instead of shopping and making new friends, I would happily make myself comfortable and dive into a book.

This is the reason why I decided to capture my imagination onto paper and begin my journey as a romance author. It is my hope that you will have enjoyed my unique romantic stories, and stay with me as I continue to pour my heart into my writing.

FREE GIFT

Sign up to my mailing list to receive an exclusive free novella, and be notified on any new releases, giveaways, contests, cover reveals and so much more!

https://dl.bookfunnel.com/kguy19f0uw

Is he just a holiday fling... or a soulmate beyond her wildest dreams?

My name is Olivia, and I've got no job, no partner, and nothing to look forward to. I could end it right there, but despite all of that, cupid works in mysterious ways.

When my girlfriends suggested a spontaneous trip to one of the most romantic cities on the planet, I could hardly refuse. The beautiful waterways of Venice might be hiding the man of my dreams... or at least they'll take my mind off my bad luck.

But I can't shake the feeling my friends are hiding something from me. I don't have much time to think about it – because now I find myself falling for someone, I never thought I would...

Is this nothing more than a holiday fling? Or could it blossom into something much more than I ever could have imagined? I guess there's only one way to find out.